MY RULES

THE LAURYN HILL STORY

At only twenty-three years old, Lauryn Hill has turned the music industry upside down and established herself as the new voice in music . . .

- *Rolling Stone* named her Best Female Artist of the Year, Best R & B Artist of the Year, and her solo debut, *The Miseducation of Lauryn Hill*, Best Album of 1998.

- *Entertainment Weekly* picked Lauryn Hill as the #1 Musical Artist of the Year.

- *The Miseducation of Lauryn Hill* debuted at #1 on the *Billboard* Music Charts, selling 400,000 copies in the first week alone.

- Lauryn Hill made history as the first female artist to win five Grammy® Awards in a single year.

And that's just the beginning . . .

MY RULES

THE LAURYN HILL STORY

Marc Shapiro

BERKLEY BOULEVARD BOOKS, NEW YORK

MY RULES: THE LAURYN HILL STORY

A Berkley Boulevard Book / published by arrangement with the author

PRINTING HISTORY
Berkley Boulevard edition / June 1999

All rights reserved.
Copyright © 1999 by Marc Shapiro.
Book design by Tiffany Kukec.
Cover design by Erika Fusari.
Cover photograph by Chris Voelker/Shooting Star.
This book may not be reproduced in whole or in part,
by mimeograph or any other means, without permission.
For information address: The Berkley Publishing Group, a
division of Penguin Putnam Inc., 375 Hudson Street,
New York, New York 10014.

The Penguin Putnam Inc. World Wide Web site address is
http://www.penguinputnam.com

ISBN: 0-425-17211-2

BERKLEY BOULEVARD
Berkley Boulevard Books are published by The Berkley Publishing Group,
a division of Penguin Putnam Inc., 375 Hudson Street,
New York, New York 10014.
BERKLEY BOULEVARD and its logo
are trademarks belonging to Penguin Putnam Inc.

PRINTED IN THE UNITED STATES OF AMERICA

10 9 8 7 6 5 4 3 2 1

This book is dedicated to my crew: wife, Nancy, daughter, Rachael, agent, Lori, mom, Selma, angels Bennie and Freida, dog, Keri, cat Bad Baby, cat Chaos. Influences: Charles Bukowski, the Doors, Kiss, Black Sabbath, Mountain, Cirith Ungol, Edgar Allan Poe, Clive Barker, Jack Kerouac, Allen Ginsberg, Patti Smith, Hunter S. Thompson and all the other creatures of the night. And finally to Lauryn Hill: props.

Contents

Acknowledgments

Research is the soul of a good biography and the path to reconstructing the life and times of Lauryn Hill was paved with solid reporting and insightful reporters.

I would like to thank Judy Levy for her memories.

The following magazines made the journey much easier: *Entertainment Weekly*, *Rolling Stone*, *Spin*, *Teen People*, *Time*, *Spice*, *Vibe*, *Essence*, *Harper's Bazaar* and *Ebony*. The following newspapers also contributed to the cause: *Los Angeles Times*, *The New York Times*, *Phoenix New Times*, *Pasadena Star News*, *The Salt Lake City Tribune*, *The Philadelphia Inquirer*, Worrall Community newspapers, the *National Enquirer* and editor Mark Hrywna. And finally, the following websites were integral in opening my eyes to all things Lauryn Hill: The Miseducation of Lauryn Hill, Wall of Sound, Music Boulevard, Amazon.com, NJO Entertainment, CD Now, MTV News and Sonic Net Music News. Props to you all.

Introduction

Lauryn Hill is the flavor of the month. But, boy! What a flavor!

There is one reason and only one reason why *My Rules: The Lauryn Hill Story* has been written. The lady is hot! Like a blowtorch! But beyond the obvious glitz and hype that goes with Lauryn Hill making it to the top, there's a story to tell—a truly compelling story.

Looks, to say the least, can be deceiving. Lauryn Hill is not one of those divas who has struggled for years in obscurity, poverty and pain before suddenly emerging magically into the big time; although she has battled some personal and professional demons that definitely qualify her to sing the blues.

Like many of our '90s bigger-than-life icons, Lauryn's ascendancy to the top has been astonishingly fast. Unless you lived around the corner from her home in South Orange, New Jersey, or in nearby Newark, where Lauryn entertained family and friends with renditions of songs by Gladys Knight, Roberta Flack and Stevie Wonder, your first inkling that Lauryn Hill was even on the planet came with the Fugees's first album, 1993's *Blunted on Reality*.

But long before her rise to stardom, Lauryn Hill had an intestinal fortitude and a rock-solid attitude that was forged in the fires of the real world. No, she didn't run with gangs, drink, do dope or blow off school. With her parents' steady hand, Lauryn Hill learned a positive reality while raised on a steady diet of virtue, truth, reality and God. However, she was no Goody Two-shoes. There would be stumbles and falls. But Lauryn Hill was quick to spring back to her feet and to have another go at life.

The result of being raised, emotionally, on the right side of the tracks is that Lauryn Hill has emerged into the light of the 1990s as the classic superwoman—singer, songwriter, producer (and when she's not busy setting the world of music on its head with monster-selling albums, insightful, progressive forays into rap and hip-hop; masterful performances and a vocal styling that is unique in its pure, haunting quality, you can throw in mother and political and social activist for good measure).

That's a lot to ask of somebody who espouses and epitomizes the '90s street kind of life. Until you realize that Lauryn Hill came into stardom with all the tools necessary to keep her head, heart and soul in place in a world often marred by compromise and sellout. The young woman is that rare mix of old school and new school. Her musical and emotional roots are as much Gladys Knight and Aretha Franklin as they are Run-D.M.C. Her worldview does not stop at the street corner but, rather, crosses that street and races gloriously around the world.

Lauryn Hill is about not being too big to give back to the community. But while she has raced toward the public life, there is always that gate that comes down when things begin to breech her own personal code of secrecy. She can be comfortable and at peace in the dark. Solitude, to Lauryn's way of thinking, is a place she can run to rather than away from. It is a privacy Lauryn has worked very hard at keeping and her defiance in the face of prying eyes succeeds only in strengthening her image as a real woman.

That Lauryn Hill has ended up with stardom is only icing on the cake. That she has accomplished everything she has accomplished in a mere twenty-three years is the result of her raw drive and ambition. But what ultimately puts Lauryn Hill high on a pedestal (a pedestal that she is most certainly uncomfortable with being placed on) is the fact that she has accomplished everything in her chosen profession and her life on her own terms.

Looking for even a hint of compromise? You

won't find it here. Personally and professionally, Lauryn Hill has played by her rules and only her rules and has come out on top.

My Rules: The Lauryn Hill Story was not written on a foundation of smoke and mirrors. If you're looking for gimmicks, this is the wrong book for you. There is no sleight of hand. Lauryn did not have to sleep her way to the top, drug her way to the top or sell her soul to the devil in any way, shape or form.

Lauryn Hill can sleep at night. And her story is the reason why.

MY RULES

THE LAURYN HILL STORY

Nobody would have batted an eye if the twenty-three-year-old singer-songwriter with the spiky dreadlocks and the polished, street-smart attitude had returned to her South Orange, New Jersey, home and had taken a year or two off to find out what being a mom was all about. Or, perhaps, decided to get out of the business altogether.

But putting her feet up and retiring from the spotlight is not what Lauryn Hill is all about.

"When some women are pregnant, their hair and nails grow," reflected Hill to *Ebony* at the time her belly was swelling and bouts with morning sickness had become an almost hourly occurrence. "But what happened to me was that my mind and the ability to create expanded."

This surge of creativity coincided with the fact that Lauryn Hill was now suddenly very much in demand. Her stint with the Fugees and the juice she received in the wake of that group's 17-million-selling album *The Score* had given the singer-songwriter an aura of respectability that few rap-hip-hop artists had received. But Arista Records A & R representative Drew Dixon had to admit that the outside world was not quick to embrace her potential in areas other than singing.

"It was tough getting people to believe that this twenty-three-year-old African-American woman best known for singing the hell out of 'Killing Me

Softly' was also a really talented songwriter and producer,'' remembered Dixon in a *Spin* magazine story.

However, respected performers who normally would not be caught dead collaborating with the cliche gangsta rappers like Ol' Dirty Bastard (of the Wu-Tang Clan) or Snoop Doggy Dogg began to see something special in Lauryn Hill. There was a sense of clean about her. She did not come across as a thug in musician's clothing. What they saw was talent, determination and a willingness to take the music the extra mile and the extra step. People who didn't know Lauryn Hill from Adam two years ago were now willing to take a chance on her and put their careers in her hands.

So much so that seven months after the Fugees's tour ended, Hill was moving very slowly and with a lot of discomfort inside a stuffy Detroit recording studio, turning the producing knobs while Aretha Franklin belted out the Hill-penned song ''A Rose Is Still a Rose'' on the other side of the glass.

Lauryn was in awe of Aretha Franklin. But she was not afraid to suggest ways to amplify those talents. Bring up the drums, sing a line a different way. These were suggestions that Lauryn made gracefully, almost childlike and always subtle. Lauryn was dealing with a legend and she knew that nothing becomes a legend more than respect.

Aretha, a seasoned pro, took those suggestions and Lauryn's way of expressing them seriously. She saw in the young woman with the swelling belly an emotional and creative equal. And in Franklin, Lauryn Hill saw the peacefulness and serenity that she wanted in her world.

But Hill was far from finished with the "First Lady of Soul." When she got wind that Franklin was hot to do a video of the song, she waddled forward and said she could direct it. Aretha was convinced Lauryn could handle it. Her record company, knowing how important it was that Aretha's latest single register with the public in a big way, was not sure. But nobody in their right mind was going to argue with this pregnant dynamo and so Hill, in a matter of weeks, added video director to her growing list of skills.

Lauryn's skills as a video director were largely instinctual. She learned the basic nuts and bolts of camera work by looking over the shoulders of the directors on the Fugees's videos. As for the rest . . . if it felt right, she went for it.

While the Aretha Franklin sessions showed true grit, what came next in Lauryn Hill's race to motherhood was downright scary.

Hill was bloated and her skin had taken an alternately flushed and pasty look as she struggled into the producer's chair and began fiddling with the recording studio's audio equipment. Gospel singer CeCe Winans had seen her come into the recording studio and was immediately at her side, inquiring in concerned tones if she was okay. Winans was feeling more than a little bit guilty. Yes, she had wanted Lauryn's skills and enthusiasm on her side. But this woman was about to have a baby, and Winans thought the last place she should be is in a recording studio. Hill smiled a tight smile and said she was fine.

Lauryn Hill was in her ninth month and the baby was due any second. But she had written the soul-stirring song for the veteran singer and had sold her on letting her produce the track. Winans saw something in Lauryn as well. Winans saw faith and she agreed to test it. Hill was not going to let any physical discomfort get in the way of her finishing the job and, in fact, as the session progressed, Winans and the assembled technicians seemed to gather strength and inspiration from the slight woman with the bulging stomach who was urging the singer, in a pained, exhausted tone of voice, on to greater and greater emotional heights. After hours of take after take, Winans and Hill were finally satisfied with the song. Hill went home and collapsed into bed.

Hours later, Lauryn went into labor and her son, Zion, was born the next day. The consensus was that

Lauryn Hill would now need to take some time off. And sure enough, for the next eight months, diaper changes, breast-feeding and being a loving mother occupied Lauryn's every waking hour. Her family and friends marveled at the way Hill was able to turn off the music world and concentrate on all things domestic. But, in those rare moments alone with her thoughts, Lauryn Hill sensed something else was going on—in her head and in her heart.

"I don't know if it was a hormonal or an emotional thing," remembered Hill in *Ebony*. "But I was suddenly very much in touch with my feelings. I suddenly had this strong desire to write."

The feelings began to pour out of Lauryn, often bringing tears to her eyes. Sometimes tears of happiness. Sometimes tears of anger and pain. And yes, there were the smiles and laughter, too. The feelings became songs.

One year later, Lauryn Hill was the *Titanic* of the pop-music world.

"For Best Album of the Year . . . Lauryn Hill! For Best R & B Album . . . Lauryn Hill! For Best New Artist . . . Lauryn Hill!"

The Grammy nominating bell would toll ten times in Lauryn Hill's name during the first week in January 1999. And most of the props were in the direction of her postpregnancy creative rush that resulted in her debut solo album, *The Mised-*

ucation of Lauryn Hill. The album was a dizzying array of fiery raps and progressive soul and jazz matings that addressed both street- and Godlike issues. It exploded onto the charts shortly after its August 1998 release immediately catapulting the twenty-three-year-old singer-songwriter into that rarefied atmosphere of superstardom. The album had already sold more than three million copies and had been named album of the year on numerous critics' lists long before the Grammy list was announced.

Lauryn Hill should have been popping the champagne corks and dancing till dawn. Instead she was sitting in the living room of her home. Being a mother.

When the Grammy nominations were announced, Lauryn was preparing to feed her three-month-old daughter, Selah Louise, who had been born November 12, 1998, and was her second child with her steady companion Rohan Marley, and chasing through her South Orange, New Jersey, house after Zion. There was the expected rush of congratulatory phone calls and, when Lauryn was able to catch her breath, she was on the phone, ironing out the particulars of her first European solo tour that was set to begin in a matter of weeks. And finally there was the quick inquiry into the status of some upcoming events of the Refugee

Project, a charity organization founded by Hill to improve the life of inner-city children.

When the dust finally settled, Lauryn did find a moment to acknowledge, in a *Pasadena Star News* story, the nominations and what they meant to her: "I think it is a strong statement, in these days, that I can make an album completely from my soul and without compromise and be acknowledged for it. Praise God."

This, then, is the nonstop world of Lauryn Hill. If you blink, you're liable to miss something. Because Lauryn Hill has more facets to her personal and professional life than any handful of diamonds.

And the first thing you notice is her beauty.

The eyes—dark, piercing and direct. The proverbial mirrors to a soul that run defiant, insistent, restless and all emotional points in between. Her body, even in its pregnant state, is cut from classic, sleek athletic lines, capable of movements quick and subtle—classic dance moves that serve to emphasize her mood and being. Then she opens her mouth. And you find out that her beauty is much more than skin-deep.

You don't get a lot of song and dance with Lauryn Hill. What you get is the truth as only Lauryn Hill can state it—straightforward, not always pretty, but always right on the money in her perception of the world and how she functions in it.

"This is a very sexist industry," the candid Hill once explained in *Essence* magazine. "Men like it when you sing to them but step out and try to control things and they have doubts."

Hill's self-evident black pride and the willingness to speak her mind made some unpleasant headlines in 1997 when, while riding the wave of success with *The Score*, she stated, in vitriolic tones, during a series of post-Grammy interviews that she would be happy if only black people bought the Fugees's albums. It was not a statement offered in haste. Lauryn Hill, while not remotely racist, pure and simple, meant every word of it. She would later offer that the statement was taken out of context and blown all out of proportion but, to her credit and integrity, she never denied that she said it.

She saw herself as a really regular person. There was to her way of thinking no empire around her.

What there is, is a largely symbiotic affinity for her roots. Lauryn can play the Hollywood game but you always get the feeling that when she's doing the party scene or the record company gladhanding that she would rather be someplace else. She is at her most comfortable around neighborhood friends and neighbors. At a time when Lauryn's name is on everyone's lips, she finds herself most often relaxed in solitude: sitting in a dimly lit living room with her children and her mother nearby or sitting on a front-porch chair surveying the block she grew up on.

"I don't like to stay away from home for long periods of time," she once confessed to *Rolling Stone*. "Your environment is what molds you. I always like to come back to the environment that brought me to a certain place."

Lauryn Hill is a fast, precise talker whose staccato bursts, in response to even the most mundane question, always seem a declaration of independence. Hill likes the sound of the word "talent" and bristles at the mention of the word "diva." Lauryn's been called a bitch behind her back, a workaholic to her face and a militant more times than she can count. Her response has been to smile, shrug and indicate it comes with the territory. For Lauryn, those descriptions are badges of honor.

Lauryn Hill is religious in a world-weary, street sort of way that makes even the most self-indulgent proclamations easy to swallow. She is detailed and conscientious in a way that belies her young years and, yes, she's smart—whip-smart. And because she is all those things and more, Lauryn Hill has been able to ride the wave of success; first as a part of the progressive hip-hop, R & B group the Fugees and now as a solo artist, with her dignity and ego fully intact.

"I actually resent superstardom," she offered in a 1998 conversation with *Vibe*. "Because with superstardom comes a lot of shit. I'm not a superstar. I don't fit the profile. I can't come into a photo shoot, rip through clothes and holler at people."

Which does not mean she is not savoring the fruits of her labors.

"I think for a hot minute this is exciting to me," she once gushed to *Harper's Bazaar* in response to how she deals with fame. "But I'm pretty much uninspired by money and material things. I pray for the things I want but I never prayed to become a superstar. I never prayed 'God! Let me sell six million records.' It just happened."

Which is why when the big money from *The Score* came rushing in, Hill's big move in the direction of luxury was to buy her parents a brand-new home and then to move back into the house she grew up in, reveling in the peace and security that being in familiar surroundings gives her. Still, Lauryn is high on fashion and when out in public she looks like a princess in the best designer clothes and stylist's do's. But in her private moments, Lauryn Hill seems to bend over backwards to hide the glamorous side, preferring boots, jeans and what she calls a "rootsy look" that, she once laughingly explained, was equal parts "Armani and army-navy."

Hill has acknowledged that she is walking a material and emotional minefield in her chosen career but feels she has what it takes to survive with her dignity and soul intact. "It's easy to get egocentric in this business," she told the *Los Angeles Times*. "But I don't think an expensive car should be at the forefront of your goals. If I can provide some comfort or encouragement or even wisdom . . . that's my goal."

Hill's real-world attitude in the often prefab celebrity-entertainment universe has made a lot of converts in a relatively short period of time. Selwyn Hides, the editor of the influential hip-hop magazine *The Source*, has praised Hill by saying "her drive and ambition are just boundless."

"She's positive, detailed and very conscientious," offered Aretha Franklin in *Harper's Bazaar* of her memories of their time together. "I was surprised to see all that in such a young woman."

Whoopi Goldberg, who starred in the film *Sister Act 2: Back in the Habit* which also featured Lauryn Hill in an early acting role, proclaimed that Lauryn was simply sublime.

Suzette Williams, who serves as treasurer of Hill's Refugee Project, has had a front-row seat to how Lauryn Hill gets through her life. Suzette likes what she's seen in her boss's enthusiasm and spontaneity. "She takes an idea and makes it happen," offers Williams in *Essence*. "She's not scared of obstacles, she's not scared of opposition, and that's rare."

Mark Bennett, who served as assistant road manager on the Fugees's *The Score* tour has gone so far as to call Lauryn the perfect black woman. She's smart, has heart and she's up front. He further stated that you always know where Lauryn is coming from.

But Lauryn Hill's life has been far from one big, free ride. Her early years were marked by constant battles between her religious upbringing and the temptations of the real world. A first serious romance in Lauryn's teen years continued to be a painful mystery that, to this day, she barely acknowledges and then only in the vaguest of terms. Other romances in what she often described as her "dysfunctional" period often found her depressed and lonely at a time when she should have been at her happiest. And finally there is that innate drive and selflessness that has always instinctively driven Hill to make other's lives easier at the expense of her own well-being.

This was something Lauryn candidly admitted to when, shortly before the birth of her second child, she acknowledged, "Going off the road because I was pregnant [with my first child] was one of the first things I did where I put my happiness first."

Unfortunately at a time when her new child and a monster of an album should have had Lauryn on cloud nine, negative circumstances have been putting a damper on the first moments of peace she has had in many years. The first blow came in December 1998 when a group of musicians who worked on *The Miseducation of Lauryn Hill* album filed a lawsuit against the singer-songwriter claiming they were owed millions of dollars in royalties for production work on the album. Her world was further rocked in January 1999 when her lover, Rohan, nearly died in a car fire.

And Lauryn's current status as a solo star on the rise has caused some doubts, and no small amount of friction between her relationship with the other two members of the Fugees. As early as the group's *Blunted on Reality* album, there were already rumblings in the industry that Lauryn ''was'' the group despite the fact that all three members made it clear that the Fugees were a communal, ''family'' effort.

Lauryn's good vibe once again came under attack when the rumors began taking root that the song ''Lost Ones'' on *The Miseducation of Lauryn Hill* was, in fact, a thinly veiled attack by Lauryn against her group mates in the Fugees and the overwhelming perception that she had surpassed them in the race to fame and fortune. This, combined with the fact that Hill had taken separate management for her solo career, spelled Trouble with a capital T.

Group member Wyclef Jean, when asked by a *Rolling Stone* reporter about the purported reference, cautiously stated "As far as I know, I don't understand why she would be talking about me on that record." David Sonenberg, the Fugees's manager, has, likewise, been cautiously optimistic that Hill is going to be able to divide her time between the group and her solo career: "I wish she felt there wasn't a conflict," he told the *Los Angeles Times*. "But I'm prepared to try and work this out."

To this point Hill has remained secretive on the subject, stating that there is no feud "but that there is some competitiveness" with the other Fugees members. She cautiously predicts a new Fugees album in 1999 or 2000. As she moves toward the end of the millennium, however, she is seemingly more intent on stretching her wings on even more non-Fugees projects. There are plans in the works for a tour with creatively like-minded soul star D'Angelo.

And while Lauryn's second pregnancy cost her a part in the critically acclaimed albeit box office disaster *Beloved*, she is definitely warming up to a second phase of her acting career. She was, for a period of time, considering a role in the film adaptation of the John Irving novel *The Cider House*

Rules, which ultimately ran afoul of her touring plans, and she has had serious discussions with the filmmakers behind the long-rumored film adaptation of the musical *Dreamgirls*. Hill has also started her own production company, Black Market Films, and is "looking for that one dope script to come along."

But for a life and career that is currently in high gear, Lauryn Hill is moving with a surprisingly laid-back attitude through her present and her future. "I think God has a plan for me," she philosophically reported in *Harper's Bazaar*. "It's like: 'Okay, Lauryn. Everything is in place. Now do what you have to do. Say what you have to say.'"

TWO

Old Soul

South Orange, New Jersey, is a place that is caught between two worlds.

When the rain lets up or the sky is cast in its eerie blue-gray-white hues, the suburban landscape of middle-class frame houses, neatly trimmed front lawns and tree-lined residential streets leap startlingly into relief, casting South Orange as the sedate, conservative city where typical middle-class families, white and black, settle in for the night.

And then there's the other side. A few hundred yards from this slice of suburbia lies the infamous urban blight of Newark where housing projects, rising nightmarishly dark and dirty into the skyline, are a breeding ground of gangs, drugs and dead-end lives. Lauryn Hill easily could have wound up here—if her parents had not had other ideas.

Originally from Haiti, Mal and Valerie Hill were no strangers to notions of poverty, racism and hopelessness. They had seen enough of it before coming to America.

Mal and Valerie had come of age in the turbulent '60s; when blacks in America were just coming out of the darkness of segregation and second-class citizenship and into the light of equal opportunity. Schools had slowly but surely been integrated. People were allowed any seat on the bus they wanted and great strides had been made toward making discrimination a thing of the past. Mal and Valerie were taking advantage of the times.

Mal had gone to college and graduated with honors with a degree that would land him a high-paying job as a computer consultant. Likewise, Valerie had pursued higher education and had turned a teaching degree into a job teaching junior high school English in nearby Newark.

Theirs was not a storybook meeting. Valerie had been coming home from a school dance one night when she ran into an out-of-breath Mal who was running for his life from a neighborhood crazy person. It was more bemusement on Valerie's part than love at first sight. But, as casual dating turned into something more serious, Mal and Valerie saw drive, ambition and the determination for a better life in each other's eyes. Love and marriage were right around the corner.

The pair had seen enough of the real world to know that they wanted only the best chance for their children and, shortly after their marriage, the couple moved to a modest frame house in South Orange.

Their first child, a son named Malaney, was born in 1973. The Hills had always felt that two children would be ideal, and that a girl would be nice. Both their wishes came true on May 25, 1975, when Lauryn Hill came screaming into the world.

Lauryn Hill was a bright, inquisitive child who, from the moment she could crawl, was into every corner of her world and gurgling with delight at every new discovery. When she began to walk, her parents were hard-pressed to keep up with her and when she started to talk, they were constantly being barraged with baby talk that always seemed to begin with the word "why."

The Hill family was well-off but not rich by any means. Mal would often moonlight as a nightclub and wedding singer to bring in extra money. Consequently Malaney and Lauryn remembered being comfortable but learning, quite naturally, to appreciate the things that money could not buy.

"I wasn't raised rich," said Hill in a 1998 interview in *Essence*. "But I never really wanted the things that we didn't have. I think my parents instilled in us that we didn't need lavish things. As long as we had love and protection we were always taken care of."

That Lauryn grew up in a close-knit family environment was an understatement. The Hills had lots of family and friends and it was not uncommon for meals to find a collection of aunts, uncles, cousins and neighborhood friends of Mal and Valerie gathered around the dining-room table. It was during these gatherings that the precocious Lauryn would wind up being the center of attention with an impromptu dance or a gymnastic flip that would elicit applause and praise.

Hill recalled in later years how those early days of ego gratification as a young child planted the seeds of ambition that took root as she grew older. Approval from others seemed to be the fuel that drove her young mind.

She has stated that as a very little girl she wanted to be a superstar/lawyer/doctor. To her way of thinking she always had an agenda.

An agenda that often centered around playtime. Valerie Hill vividly remembered in a *Teen People* feature coming home from work to find "Lauryn curled up on her bed, playing and singing to her dolls."

The education of Lauryn Hill was fueled, to a large extent, by her parents. Mal and Valerie knew that it was important that their children take advantage of their recent strides away from segregation. So they willingly sent their children to the nearby elementary school, which was largely white. But they were also intent on teaching Malaney and Lauryn about black studies and the importance of keeping in touch with their black roots. The result was that Lauryn spent just as much time running around the white suburban streets as she did playing in and around the Newark housing projects. There was never any fear on her parents' part that spending any time in the ghetto would be harmful. As a result, Lauryn felt comfortable in both worlds.

"I always had this duality," she related in a 1996 conversation with *Rolling Stone*. "I went to school with a lot of white kids in a really suburban environment. But I lived with black kids and white kids. Plus my whole family lives in Newark, in the city. So I grew up with two kinds of people in my life."

Lauryn's penchant for being on stage and the center of attention began to be apparent by age three. With the Jackson Five constantly blaring out of the family radio, the young child became totally enamored of Michael Jackson and could be counted on to improvise a wildly exaggerated dance routine to the song "ABC" every time Lauryn heard it. Lauryn also went through a phase where she was captivated by the Brooke Shields Calvin Klein commercial and once reduced her family to tears of laughter when she put on a ballet outfit and seductively intoned the tag line "Nothing comes between me and my Calvins."

"If we had the camcorder out, she was ready," Valerie Hill laughingly recalled in *Spin* magazine. "She was very clear about her future, even then."

Lauryn's childhood antics began to solidify into a more concrete plan by the time she turned six. A lot of Lauryn's early experiments with singing were obviously childlike in nature and, more often than not, laughably off-key. But Lauryn was persistent, often frowning at a vocal misstep and then plowing ahead until she got it right. Her overly theatrical attempts at singing were, through trial and error, beginning to take on a more measured, soulful tone. She felt that what made her decide to sing was that she decided that she knew what she wanted to hear.

She would often come upon her father singing in preparation for a nightclub date and join in for a duet that would eventually have the entire Hill clan dissolving into waves of laughter.

The precocious child was also quick to enlist neighborhood kids in her singing games, forming impromptu groups that attempted to sound like the favorite radio hits of the day. "We had so many names for those groups that I don't even remember them all," Lauryn laughed at the memory in a *Rolling Stone* conversation. "I was always very dramatic. I was very ridiculous. You know how it is when you're just happy to sing."

In private conversations, Mal and Valerie sensed that their daughter had the instincts to be a performer, and that she was taking the whole idea of performing very seriously for somebody so young. The parents made a pact to support their daughter in her desire to perform as long as her aspirations did not interfere with her education.

"When she was a little girl I took Lauryn to see *Annie* in the city," related Valerie Hill to *Essence*. "Afterward Lauryn asked me if there could ever be a black *Annie*."

Valerie Hill indicated to her young daughter that she did not see why not. But while Broadway was on her mind that day, and the Hill household echoed with the sounds of Lauryn warbling the song "Tomorrow" for quite a while after that day, Lauryn Hill's real musical education began the day the young girl, then age seven, was rummaging around in the basement and found a literal treasure trove of six hundred old, scratchy forty-fives by such classic Motown, Stax Volt, Philadelphia International performers such as Gladys Knight, Curtis Mayfield, Roberta Flack and Donny Hathaway, as well as an odd assortment of rock singles by the likes of Santana. Many of the records were so old that they still had her mother's name on them from when she was in high school. And while there had "always been music in the house," this was the first time Lauryn had some treasures she could call her own.

She immediately ran upstairs and brought down her toy carryall record player. The tiny sound of some of the classics of the '60s and '70s was soon reverberating off the basement walls and ceiling. But the basement was not the most comfortable place to listen to music, so Lauryn eventually gathered up an armful of her mother's old records, carried them upstairs and began playing them on the family's record player.

Lauryn spent hours carefully placing the records on the spindle, dropping the needle carefully on the edge and just as carefully removing them when she was finished, barely making a dent in any record. Some of the records had audible scratches and pops. But for Lauryn, "they were the most beautiful thing I had ever heard."

Those records became her musical theory teacher. The lyrics that really stood out for her were heartfelt and hurtful. Lauryn was listening to things like Nina Simone and Stevie Wonder and feeling like she wanted to cry. She was listening to singers like Al Green and Sam Cooke. Lauryn could feel the power of their voices.

Something in those time-honored crooners and the way they worked their magic with a song hit Lauryn hard—real hard. She began spending all her free moments singing along with them and moving, her eyes closed in ecstasy, to the rhythm of those dusty old records. Many were the nights that, long after she was supposed to be in bed, Lauryn would gather up an armful of records, bring them to her room, put on headphones and groove to the music until early morning. It was not uncommon for Valerie Hill to peek into her daughter's bedroom at one o'clock in the morning only to find Lauryn curled up asleep with earphones on her head. But Lauryn remembered that differently, recalling in *Spin* that she rarely got the records up to her room.

"I haven't slept in my bed since 1986 or '87. I got these big-ass headphones with leather cushions and went to sleep listening to the music."

Lauryn would listen to the records endlessly: first as a fan, but eventually the child would begin mentally to dissect each song in an attempt to find out what made them tick. She found herself developing an ear for live strings and live instrumentation and an appetite for certain sounds.

When she felt confident, she would often entertain her family and friends with interpretations of the classic '60s singers. Ever the critic, Hill laughingly recalled those early singing sessions in a 1998 *Rolling Stone* interview. "I was a performer since I was little," she said, "but I think I'm less of a performer now than when I was a child. Back then, I was such a ham. I was so dramatic."

Lauryn Hill had found something she loved and that love eventually developed into an encyclopedic knowledge of the music of the '60s and '70s. She was the kid at the family barbecues in the middle of Newark listening to the oldies station with the old folks. They'd go 'Oh, that's Blue Magic!' And Lauryn would respond with 'No, it's the Chi-Lites.' Or they'd go 'Who wrote the song "Hypnotized"?' And Lauryn would be like 'Linda Jones— 1967.' "

The Hill household continued to be a place that was alive with music. Mal continued to moonlight as a nightclub and wedding singer. Valerie studied piano and Malaney played guitar, sax and drums.

Lauryn's first instrument of choice was the violin. Even at that early age, there was a passion in her playing that impressed her teacher, who gushed to Valerie that she "did not believe how musical she is." Valerie was not surprised, having long ago realized that Lauryn "just had this effect on people who listened to her," recalled Valerie in a *Los Angeles Times* story.

Her confidence soaring, Lauryn made a fateful decision at age thirteen. She had heard that the television series *Showtime at the Apollo* occasionally allowed amateurs to sing on the show. With her parents' support, Lauryn auditioned for and was picked to sing on an upcoming show.

On the day of the show, Lauryn's parents rented a van, filled it with Lauryn's friends and drove off to the Apollo. The song Lauryn had chosen to sing was Smokey Robinson's "Who's Lovin' You." Lauryn was confident as she stood in the wings, awaiting her turn. But when the time came for her to step onstage, she took one look out into the packed theater and panicked.

She stepped to the mike. As she began to sing, however, she began inching away from the microphone. As her voice faded, boos began to rain down on Lauryn from the audience. She was like a deer caught in the headlights. Lauryn wanted to run off stage and hide. But fear kept her rooted in that spot.

Suddenly, from amid the boos, a loud, shrill command caught Lauryn's attention. It was Valerie's brother-in-law screaming, "Get close to the mike!" The words shocked the young girl back to her senses. She stepped forward, grabbed the mike and began singing like a girl possessed. Lauryn's turnaround was greeted with deafening applause and screams of support.

She was elated after her performance but her mood was quiet on the van ride home. Valerie sensed what her daughter was feeling.

Lauryn was crushed. Yes, she had turned the audience around with a spirited, emotional performance. But the perfectionist in her was not satisfied. In her mind she had let herself down. Lauryn started to cry. Valerie sat down with her daughter when they arrived home and supportively told her the facts of life. She told her daughter that some days people might clap for her and some days they might not.

"This is part of the business that you say you want to be in," she recalled telling Lauryn in a *Rolling Stone* article. "Now, if every time they don't scream and holler you're gonna cry, then perhaps this isn't for you."

Lauryn sniffed, wiped her eyes and stared defiantly at her mother. She looked at her mother like she was crazy. To her, the mere suggestion that music wasn't for her was insane."

Lauryn had a much more pleasant experience when, while still in junior high school, she was invited to sing the national anthem at the nearby

Columbia High School basketball game. LuElle Walker-Peniston, who would serve as Hill's guidance counselor at Columbia years later, recalled Hill's rendition with obvious glee in *Time* magazine. "People went wild. She was inspiring. Fans liked her rendition so much that recordings of it were played at subsequent games."

Lauryn would occasionally be taunted by her teen friends who, at the time, were listening to the hip '80s sounds of Duran Duran and New Edition while she continued to be transfixed by the hits of the past. But for the most part, her outgoing nature and the ability to make friends easily found her never far from a group of kids and an ever-widening circle of friends.

"When I was this kid, I was this sort of bright and shining kid who had a real pure heart and pure spirit," she told *Rolling Stone*. "I was real crazy. Everything I did was dramatic. I was wild."

Lauryn, by this time, had developed a healthy ego—one that would occasionally get out of control. Hill was confident to the point where she quite literally felt she was invincible and that nothing was beyond her grasp.

Miriam Farrakahn, a childhood friend, painfully remembered in *Essence* how one day Lauryn's ego nearly cost her her life. "A bunch of us went swimming and Lauryn swore up and down that she could swim. I mean, she was trying to tell us how to swim. So, we were like 'Okay, let's see how you dive.' We threw her in and she almost drowned. Literally almost drowned.''

But far from being the proverbial wild child, Lauryn's upbringing was tempered by a healthy dose of religion. She gladly dressed for Sunday church services and could be heard singing out the hymns and prayers from her place in a center row. When Lauryn was younger, she felt very close to God.

And it was her belief in God that allowed this headstrong child to adopt what would be a lifelong path of patience, understanding and optimism when it came to her encounters outside the four walls of her South Orange home.

Lauryn would often look out her bedroom window onto the Newark housing projects; the bleakness and depression of that dead-end part of town. But as she looked, the inevitable silver lining would pop into her head.

''I remember looking out this window, and there was a certain time of day when the sun used to shine on those buildings she told *Rolling Stone*. They used to look like gold. Beautiful. And I'd bug 'cause I knew they were full of wild people, kids stickin' up each other. But when something is at its worst, there's always something beautiful there, too.''

THREE

Life Lessons

Lauryn Hill entered Columbia High School in 1990 with all the confidence and cockiness expected of most fifteen-year-olds. There was a big, wide world out there and Lauryn was certain that she was going to conquer it.

"She had a very good head on her shoulders," acknowledged Columbia High School communications coordinator Judy Levy. Levy, who recalled, in a 1999 conversation, Lauryn's active involvement in the school's theater productions, The Martin Luther King Association and the gospel choir, reflected that Lauryn was consistent in her ability to balance things out. "She was a very good student and the main thing was that she was involved in a lot of things, which is what made her a good student. Whatever she did, she just fit right in.''

Lauryn's parents had continued to emphasize the importance of education through her junior high school years, the result of which had been Lauryn entering her freshman year with exceptionally high grades and moving on the immediate fast track to honors-level classes. And what her teachers found was a student who adjusted to and was comfortable with the academic side of life while, at the same time, being socially well adjusted. LuElle Walker-Peniston, the school's guidance counselor, agreed in a Worrall Community newspaper article with Levy's assessment. ''Lauryn was an excellent student who took advantage of opportunities.'' Lauryn, while avoiding any serious teen romantic relationships, was quite popular.

Mal Hill would find out just how popular when he and his daughter sat down to discuss the particulars of her fifteenth birthday party. He recalled that Lauryn had asked if she could have her birthday party in the backyard. He told her yes but only to invite her closest friends. Mal was shocked when by the end of the night 250 people must have showed up.

Hill continued to have a love affair with singing but was cautious in approaching it with a career in mind. She would sing in impromptu jams at school and at her home but never had she made any mention about a desire to turn professional, at least not publicly. Acting was a whole other matter. Her natural charm and ability to sing with feeling made acting a natural adjunct to her singing, so Mal and Valerie Hill were not surprised the day their daughter came to them and said she wanted to act and begin going out on auditions. They supported her decision—up to a point.

"We made a deal," stated her mother to the *Los Angeles Times* in 1998, looking back on the day. "I said that, as long as her schoolwork came first, I would be happy to chauffeur her to auditions and showcases. And she kept up her end of the bargain."

While Lauryn was pursuing academic and creative excellence in the suburbs of South Orange, a couple of brothers from across the river were also attempting to get their acts and lives together.

Prakazrel "Pras" Michel, born in the Crown Heights section of Brooklyn, was a teen who could go either way. Despite a sheltered home life, a natural curiosity and a high IQ, Michel, a realist with his eye always on the prize or the money, had his run with gangs in his early teens and seemed destined to play in the gangsta life to the bitter end.

"I had a gun put in my mouth while someone threatened to pull the trigger," he recalled almost matter-of-factly to the *Los Angeles Times*. "I've been shot at and all that. I was so stupid, fighting for a block that I didn't even own.''

Fortunately for Michel, his parents decided that the safest place for their family was across the river in New Jersey, so Michel entered Lauryn Hill's Columbia High School as a senior at the same time that Hill was entering as a freshman. Prakazrel appeared to take to the change of environment. He maintained high grades, made nongangster friends and stayed out of trouble.

Wyclef "Clef" Jean was also living the life of the street. Possessing an intense, inquisitive personality even as a child, Jean, the son of a preacher and the grandson of a voodoo priest, immigrated with his family from Haiti to Brooklyn at the age of nine. Soon after his arrival in the United States, Jean began to chafe at the idea of being housed with nine other family members in a one-room apartment in a Coney Island housing project, and soon turned to the streets. By age twelve, he already had the beginnings of a juvenile rap sheet—shoplifting, cutting classes and consorting with gang types—and appeared headed down the road to destruction.

In a desperate attempt to keep her son off the streets, Jean's mother bought him a cheap, beat-up acoustic guitar and a cousin taught him his first primary chords. There was something in the idea of patiently picking complex progressions and the sweet sounds they made that appealed to the young boy. The guitar saved Jean from the streets but his love for the primitive leanings of rap music immediately put him at odds with his father. The youngster got around his father's "no rap, no hip-hop" edict by bringing home tapes of '70s progressive rock groups like Yes and Pink Floyd and passing them off as religious music.

His love of music allowed Jean to get through high school, which made his parents happy. He paid just enough attention to his studies to get by, and was in a number of informal music groups, including occasional jams with his cousin Pras Michel; honing his skills as a rapper with a more worldly, progressive edge.

He quickly moved beyond the basics of the then-popular form of gangsta rap and began seeing infinite possibilities in the form. Jean's parents were less than thrilled when he announced, near the end of his senior year in high school, that he was going to be a rock star.

True to his word, Jean signed a recording contract with tiny Big Beat Records shortly before graduating and recorded the song "Out in the Jungle," which became a regional New York hit. But when the dust settled, the success of "Out in the Jungle" had only succeeded in spurring Jean on to the next big thing.

Michel had this thing about boy-girl singing groups. He hated them. However, that had not stopped him from hooking up with a singer named Marcy and, later, was considering another sister for the group. "I had this brilliant idea that two girls and one nigga would be the bomb shit. But I didn't like the second girl's attitude and so we cut her loose," he told *Vibe*.

However, he had been hearing the buzz, through Marcy, that there was this freshman named Lauryn Hill who could sing like nobody's business. He was initially not thrilled that she was young: "I was like, 'What?'" he recalled in *Spin*. "But Marcy was persistent. She kept saying 'this girl can sing. She's baaad!'"

Michel knew Lauryn's brother, Malaney, and so an introduction was quickly arranged. Lauryn liked Michel's enthusiasm and confidence. And her already sharp instincts told her that he was sincere in looking for nothing more than a singing partner. For Michel, the feeling was mutual. He felt she was cool. In a creative sense he felt her vibe.

Michel had already set up informal headquarters in a serviceable West Orange, New Jersey, recording studio called House of Music. And it was there that Lauryn, for the first time, got an idea of what a professional singing life could be about. In consort with Michel and Marcy, the trio would regularly convene at the House of Music and lay down vocals over rap and progressive soul tracks. Lauryn was immediately comfortable with the free-swinging style of hanging out at a real recording studio and was rewarded when she was quite readily accepted into the group.

The trio had evolved into a cohesive unit and Lauryn could feel the rush as she would step forward in the recording studio to lay down soft and angry vocals like a polished professional and then dissolve into laughter when she would hear her voice played back. The dream of becoming a singer was coming together in Lauryn Hill's mind but, at the moment, she reflected it was nothing but fun.

The music was sounding good. It was sounding better than good. Lauryn, Marcy and Pras agreed that it was time to take the next serious step and give their group a name. Those early tracks had been a hybrid sound in which they rapped in different languages. They had coined the phrase "tranzlator rap" to describe what they were doing, so it seemed logical to name their group Tranzlator Crew. A buzz soon made its way through House of Music and out into the burgeoning neighborhood music scene that this group of kids was really hot. Musician and occasional House of Music producer Khalis Bayyan was one of the earliest people to catch their vibe and would regularly stop by just to listen. He could tell in his gut that Tranzlator Crew was destined for bigger and better things.

In the meantime another hot group called Exact Change, featuring Wyclef Jean, was beginning to make noise on the local hip-hop front. But Jean, while intent on following up his Big Beat Records success with an Exact Change deal, was surprisingly fluid in exploring any and all musical opportunities.

"I always used to meet up with Clef at church in Jersey," remembers Pras in *Vibe*. "He would say 'Yo man, when I get a record deal, I'm gonna put you on board.'"

But while Wyclef's deal was slow in developing, Clef would regularly get an earful from Pras about how his hot new crew was the bomb. Finally Wyclef's curiosity about what his cousin Pras was doing with Tranzlator Crew got the better of him. He just had to stop by the House of Music and check it out.

"Basically I came to check out the girls," laughed Jean in a 1996 *Rolling Stone* interview. "Pras was like 'I got two really fine babes, man.' I was there right after church in my best suit."

Jean agreed that the "two babes" were fine and his roving eye immediately sized up Lauryn for some possible dating. But while contemplating whether or not to make a move, Jean listened to the group run through some songs and he had to admit that he liked what they were doing. So much so that when his cousin suggested that Wyclef do a freestyle rap over one of their tracks, he gave it a shot.

The impact was immediate. There was a haunting, deliberate, intense feel to Jean's vocals that added an even tougher, more thought-provoking element to the group's overall sound. The other members heard the difference. But it took Bayyan, who happened to be around that day, to step forward enthusiastically and suggest that Jean join Translator Crew. Jean was not sure but agreed to sit in with the group occasionally while continuing with Exact Change. The rest of the group agreed that having Wyclef on board was the bomb.

It was during those early days in Tranzlator Crew that Lauryn began to get into the whole style of hip-hop. She liked the sense of freedom of expression and the fact that things did not have to be done a certain way. She also liked the fact that the music could be raw one instant and thoughtful and light the next.

Lauryn, in later years, would claim that she had always had an affinity for the music, even before joining Tranzlator Crew. However, David Sonenberg, the Fugees's manager, said "Lauryn was indoctrinated into hip-hop culture by Clef. But he was quick to acknowledge that nobody was going to argue with her side of the story.

As Tranzlator Crew began taking on a more professional look and sound, the hours in the studio became longer and Lauryn was, at the tender age of fifteen, pushed into a near round-the-clock schedule that she willingly embraced. "We used to be in the studio from the time after school or track practice until like three in the morning," Lauryn recalled in *Rolling Stone* of those marathon-paced days. "Then I'd go home, go to sleep, wake up at seven and go to school again."

Jean remembered those early days a lot more painfully. When he would come back from the studio, he would get a whipping from his dad because he was playing what his dad considered devil music.

The ensuing months brought a lot of changes into the lives of Tranzlator Crew. Marcy had decided to leave music behind and go off to college. Wyclef left Exact Change and joined his cousin and Lauryn full time. Pras, in the meantime, had managed to come through high school with a 3.8 grade-point average, which made him a prime candidate for the top universities. He was ultimately accepted at Yale but turned down the offer to attend college locally at Rutgers University where he would study philosophy and psychology.

Lauryn's insistence that she could act eventually began to yield success. Shortly before her sixteenth birthday, she landed the role of Kirsta Johnson on the long-running television soap opera *As the World Turns*. It was a hectic year for the young teen. It was not uncommon for the typical shooting day to last twelve hours or more. Lauryn learned about sitting around and waiting for hours for five minutes of actual work. Of course, there were her studies, which she kept up with an on-set tutor when she was working.

Lauryn's year on *As the World Turns* opened Lauryn's eyes to the reality of show biz, but it only made her all the more determined to succeed. That year included such high points as a storyline that had her in romantic clinches with actor Michael Swan and a memorable sequence in which Lauryn's character taught veteran actress Helen Wagner how to rap.

The producers were thrilled with Lauryn's natural abilities and were ready to renew her contract for another year. But Mal and Valerie felt that Lauryn was too young to make that kind of commitment to acting at the expense of a formal, and normal, education. Lauryn did not protest too much and left the show at the end of 1991.

In 1991, Hill also landed the role of rebellious Catholic school girl Rita Watson in the movie *Sis-*

ter Act 2: Back in the Habit, playing opposite Whoopi Goldberg. The role was designed as a second-tier acting part but, as Lauryn got deeper into the acting process, she began to make the character her own. Director Bill Duke saw something special in Lauryn and so, rather than follow the script to the letter, he allowed her to play around and improvise with the role of Rita. Duke, in particular, remembered the day when a pretty straightforward classroom scene turned into something extra when Lauryn approached Duke with the idea of having Rita entertain the class with an impromptu rap. ''None of that was scripted,'' he said in *Time*. ''That was all Lauryn. She was amazing.''

It was also during that period that Lauryn and Wyclef appeared, briefly, in an off-Broadway, hip-hop version of Shakespeare's *Twelfth Night* called *Club 12*. It was a marvel to family and friends alike that the group could manage to keep so many balls in the air. Lauryn, who often ended up doing her homework in the bathrooms of New Jersey clubs before the shows, looked back and wondered how they managed to keep up that grueling schedule and found a simple answer: They didn't party much, they were not taking drugs and they were working very hard.

But she was spending more time with Wyclef and the feelings between the pair were beginning to cross the line from professional to personal. Those who observed the pair saw a mild flirtation but never anything approaching a serious romance. It was as if the pair instinctively knew that to cross that line would ultimately destroy the group.

Not long after Wyclef joined the group, Tranzlator Crew began playing out for the first time. Their first shows were school talent shows and neighborhood showcases. There was rarely more than gas money on the line, but Lauryn looked back fondly on those days when they let it all hang out.

''We sang, we rapped, we danced,'' she reflected in *Rolling Stone*. ''As a matter of fact, we were a circus troupe. Maybe we were a little overdeveloped in the sense that we did so much that we were just like 'Yo, okay, I can do anything.' We were a piece of work but you could see the talent.''

The two cousins and Lauryn were spending every waking hour together, and rumors that romance was in the air and that things were running particularly hot and heavy between Lauryn and Wyclef began to surface once again. To this day, Lauryn remains tantalizingly vague on the subject of a romance, imagined or otherwise, with Wyclef.

''All of us in the group were very close,'' she told *Vibe*. ''We were a dynamic group in the sense that all of us grew up together. So there was a lot of love there.''

The slow but sure evolution of Tranzlator Crew saw Lauryn beginning to take more and more of a center stage when it came to singing. Hers was a supple instrument, capable of breathtaking leads and subtle, mercurial backups. Whether on a conscious or a subconscious level, Pras and Wyclef, who were more than capable of taking the mike when a song warranted it, seemed to take a step back, preferring to scat rap and play the edgy, subtle equivalent of Lauryn's lead.

Tranzlator Crew had adopted an attitude of family early on—all for one and one for all. But the reality was, even in these early stages, Lauryn had moved to the forefront and was not to be moved.

Pras conceded that if Lauryn wasn't there, they wouldn't be what they were now. He noted that they might have been successful, but it would have been a whole different thing.

Lauryn Hill turned seventeen amid a flurry of activity. She had managed to maintain a high grade-point average through high school and while preparing to enter her senior year, she already had the ear of such prestigious universities as Yale, Columbia, Spelman, University of Pennsylvania and Rutgers. Lauryn was leaning toward Columbia because it would keep her in New York and near her crew, which was getting anxious to crash the big time.

The group's reputation as a growing, potentially big-time act had attracted the attention of a New York manager named David Sonenberg who, typically, had promised Lauryn, Pras and Wyclef the moon. Atypically David was proving to be as good as his word. He pushed Tranzlator Crew to put together a grade-A demo tape, which he dutifully sent out to all the major record labels, inviting members of the A & R department to come to the manager's Manhattan office and see the group perform live.

Lauryn was nervous the night before the group's first audition. She knew they were good. But she was also hesitant and, perhaps, just a little bit sad that they were taking a step forward from relative innocence that they could never take back. But those concerns did not stop her from being up bright and early the next morning and making the trek into the Big Apple.

To this day, manager Sonenberg bursts out laughing when he thinks about the first time his charges strutted their stuff for the record companies. Pras was doing this rapping thing while Clef was playing guitar and rapping real wild in different languages.

"Then Lauryn was singing this soulful version of 'Imagine,'" he recalled in *Spin*. "I think it was all too much. These record company guys thought it was some weird stunt. You could see them thinking 'Is it R & B or is it rap?' They should have been thinking that it was both.''

Wyclef recalled in *Rolling Stone* that the auditions as exercises in craziness that made him frustrated. ''I was taking my shirt off, screaming out of my lungs and jumping on top of a table, going crazy. We were scaring most of these people.'' The result of the label auditions was that a lot of people were impressed, a few went so far as to predict they would be the next big thing. But ultimately, sighed Wyclef, ''Everybody came and left.''

Everybody except Ruffhouse Records. Ruffhouse had built a reputation in the music industry as an upstart label with guts that had made its name by releasing such daring acts as Cypress Hill. Ruffhouse saw the same potential in Tranzlator Crew. They liked what they saw and heard and so, by the time Lauryn Hill was celebrating her eighteenth birthday and getting ready to go off to Columbia University to get down with freshman history and English, Tranzlator Crew was signing on the bottom line of their first recording contract.

F O U R

Down with This

They were partying down in South Orange the
night Lauryn, Wyclef and Pras linked up with
Ruffhouse. Lauryn, who typically made time during the celebration to hit the books, felt she was in
a state of grace. And for the first time, she was also
feeling creatively conflicted. The idea of a group
dynamic had always seemed the ideal situation for
her. But constant performing at center stage and an
increasing involvement in the writing and behind-
the-scenes work involved in producing the demo
that landed the band with Ruffhouse had begun to
work on Lauryn's ego.

Lauryn was definitely not ready to go solo. But
she had to admit in a *Vibe* feature that part of her
was really craving the spotlight. ''There's a lot of

shared energy here,'' she admitted in a not-too-veiled reference to those early days. ''It was very important for my brothers to shine and, for a period of time, I was almost afraid to shine. But I don't feel that way anymore.''

However, Lauryn managed to put aside those thoughts of going solo amid the excitement of signing with Ruffhouse, a Pennsylvania-based independent label with all-important ties to Columbia Records. There was a flurry of excitement: papers to sign, including a production contract that would allow the label to handpick their producers; studio time to secure; and the writing of songs that would end up being on their first album. During this period the group reflected the bluster and bravado of youth. The music was their thing and nobody was going to take it away from them.

But despite hanging tough on having an individual musical identity, Tranzlator Crew had suddenly found themselves going soft when it came to demanding their rights. They were aware that their bold intentions might be compromised beneath a batch of contract clauses and ''oh, by the ways'' being uttered by their record company. However, the exuberance of youth blinded them to all but one overriding truth: ''They wanted to make a record real bad and they were willing to play by anybody's rules in order to get that first record made.

The Fugees strut their stuff at the 1996 MTV
Video Music Awards.

The Fugees with music legend Roberta Flack at the
1996 MTV Movie Awards.

Lauryn with bandmate Wyclef Jean at the
MTV Movie Awards.

The three superstars at the 1997 American
Music Awards.

Lauryn shows off her award at the *Billboard*
Music Awards, 1998.

Lauryn is every inch the beauty in her Armani
gown at the 30th NAACP Image Awards.

Photo by Miranda Shen/© 1998 by Celebrity Photo Agency, Inc.
All rights reserved.

Lauryn captivates the audience of the 41st annual Grammy® Awards.

No one can take their eyes off Lauryn Hill.

Lauryn can't help but smile after winning a record
five Grammy® Awards.

But before they could record or do anything else, for that matter, there were a couple of bumps in the road that had to be navigated. Pras, already a junior at Rutgers University, was finding it tough to balance academics and a burgeoning music career and therefore, shortly after the group signed with Ruffhouse, he dropped out of school to devote all his energies to the group.

A second annoyance occurred when a new wave rock group named Translator surfaced with the threat of a lawsuit, claiming that they had had the name first. The group held a meeting and came up with a way to avoid a legal battle. They added Fugee, short for Refugee and consistent with their philosophical and social worldview, to their moniker and became Fugee Tranzlator Crew.

By the time they entered the House of Music to record their debut album *Blunted on Reality* in 1991, the group had decided to eliminate ''Tranzlator Crew'' altogether and simply call themselves the Fugees.

''Refugees was always a negative thing,'' said Wyclef of the renaming process in *Rolling Stone*. ''We wanted to make something positive of it.''

Lauryn, in the *Los Angeles Times*, was philosophical about the name change. ''We call ourselves Fugees because we seek refuge in our music. Everybody is seeking refuge from something . . . their jobs, the ghetto, whatever.''

The Fugees, in their formative stages, saw their music as something universal and expansive; a complex mixture of gloss and primitive stylings, attitudes and messages that, from its inception, seemed to fly in the face of the prevailing musical attitudes of the day, especially as they pertained to black music in general and rap in particular. They would often joke about the crotch-grabbing and profanity-laden lyrics that had become almost cliche in rap and how they were going to take the music in a whole different direction.

When Ruffhouse signed them based on their demo tape, they figured creatively they were home free. Especially since one of their mentors from the House of Music days, Khalis Bayyan, would be among the producing crew that included such hard-core rap hip-hop veterans as Rashad Muhammad, Le Jam Productions, Brand X, Stephen Walker and Jerry.

The Fugees did not know it, but they were about to be betrayed.

Once in the studio, the trio was constantly being bombarded, by one producer or another, with suggestions aimed at turning the group into just another gangsta clone for the perceived urban rap market. The ambush was cold and calculating. Slowly but surely the group's more subtle, ambitious lyrics were replaced by an aggressive, largely cliche rhyming style. The musical mixes were sped up. A perfectly good rendition of the song "Nappy Heads" was ruined when a totally unnecessary and inappropriate sampling of a Kool and the Gang song was added.

The group managed to salvage some self-respect when Wyclef was allowed to produce—his way— the song "Vocab," a haunting piece of music in which the trio rapped eloquently over a simple acoustic guitar passage. That song *was* the Fugees. The rest of the album, in their mind, was cold, sterile and unfeeling. In fact, the only one remotely satisfied with the ways things were going was Lauryn, whose maturity as a vocalist of amazing sensuality was moved further up in the mix, albeit in a largely conventional manner.

There was anger and frustration on the Fugees's faces as they continued to work on an album that, not even halfway through the recording sessions, they already perceived as an album that did not show them off in their true light. Adversity, however, only succeeded in drawing the group closer together. Lauryn, Pras and Wyclef took every opportunity to defend their turf and occasionally the production team that was banging them would back down. However, their suggestions usually ended up being considered and just as quickly discarded in favor of obvious licks that would make them just another head in the rap herd.

"We had no clout," remembered Wyclef of that nightmarish experience in *Rolling Stone*. "They [the producers] was like 'You got to be more aggressive, you got to scream! Listen to Onyx!'"

But there was also much that was positive coming out of the sessions. The group identity that the Fugees had maintained before landing the record deal had intensified under the pressure of recording. Ideas flowed freely between the trio and decisions that made the final cut were group decisions. At the end of the day they had proven to themselves that they could ride out the storm.

An interesting dynamic began to form during those sessions. Pras seemed to gravitate more and more toward the technical-production side of things. Lauryn and Wyclef, who according to reports from the studio, were continuing their mild flirtation, both had songwriting in their souls and soon found themselves in friendly competition to see who could come up with the best lyrics or the baddest rhyme.

With the completion of *Blunted on Reality*, the Fugees hunkered down in their emotional bunker and waited for the bombs to fall. They would have a long wait.

Internal problems immediately began to develop within Ruffhouse and between Ruffhouse and the parent company, Columbia Records. The main problems centered on a professional difference of opinion between Columbia-Ruffhouse executives Chris Schwartz and Joe Nicolo and, unfortunately, spread to every facet of the group's debut disc. Everything from tour plans to which single should be released first to promotion became major contention points between the group's management and the record company. Release dates for the album were scheduled, canceled and rescheduled. Weeks dragged into months and finally into years. It would be two years before *Blunted on Reality* found its way into record shops.

The album was finally released in 1993 and received a decidedly mixed reception. The record, surprisingly, went down quite well in Europe where listeners, not yet fully indoctrinated into the intricacies of rap, were able to weed through the obvious cliches and see that something new and different was percolating between the grooves.

American audiences, on the other hand, were downright nasty in dismissing the album out of hand. Admittedly, *Blunted on Reality* was an easy target for critics as the Fugees's strong lyrical bent and imaginative approach to the music sank in the mire of questionable production. The album that finally hit the streets was wildly overproduced, the songs sounding surprisingly dated given the group's vaunted progressive edge and there was an overriding sense of condescension that angered listeners more than it entertained. The hip-hop and rap press was particularly nasty, offering that the Fugees were just the latest group to try to cash in on hard-core rap and had the distinction of completely missing the point.

But there were some perceptive reviews that made it clear that people were seeing the potential beneath the shoddy mix. The *New York Times* offered that the album contained ''brash, smart raps, drawing on Jamaican dance hall rhythms as well as American hip-hop.'' *Vibe* kicked in with, ''The Fugees are talented songwriters and gifted rappers.'' *The Source*, in praising the album, also took an early shot at highlighting Lauryn when it said, ''Lauryn possesses much of the trio's lyrical muscle. She steals the show again and again on every track she appears on.'' And finally *Melody Maker*, the influential British music paper, brazenly acknowledged the album as ''a fine point at which to recapture the time when black Americans didn't have to act like f——ing criminals to turn whitey on.''

The Fugees were grateful for the good notices but the group still felt thoroughly blindsided by the experience of recording the album. Consequently they risked the anger of their record label by stating, to anyone who would listen, that their vision had, to a large degree, been compromised by their producers and, by association, their record label. Lauryn, in particular, pulled no punches in defending their creative goals against the corporate establishment. She stated that hip-hop kids wanted their music to be real and that record companies were only interested in getting one side across.

She also took the opportunity in *Vibe* to acknowledge that, although it did not completely come across in *Blunted on Reality*, the Fugees were part of a new wave of performers dedicated to destroying what she perceived as a false image: "It's become popular to be stupid, to be violent, to be unintelligent and that's bad. When people stop being who they are naturally and start pretending to be something negative or not real, that's what's wack."

Lauryn continued her studies at Columbia University. She had to juggle her schedule, which included extended studies in Spanish and being the tri-captain of the Columbia University cheerleading squad, so that the Fugees could do some touring in support of the album. It was in those instances when audiences caught the group live that the real potential of the Fugees came into view.

Once again, the inexperienced Fugees caved in to management pressures and went on stage in color-coordinated outfits and performed embarrassing between-song dance routines. However, performing live seemed to have a freeing aspect as they traded vocals and instruments and glossed over the obvious elements of rap and hip-hop with a fresh, progressive sheen. In fact, after coming offstage to supportive but not overly enthusiastic applause, the group's members would often speculate why their first album had not been a live one.

Lauryn, during this period, speculated on the reality of that first recording experience and attempted to put a positive spin on it. "I had very little creative input in that first album. I was just happy to be on the record. What that first album did for us was to give us the exposure and the education. We were smart enough to pay very close attention to how to perform, how to self-promote and just how to make music."

Blunted on Reality sold moderately well, an estimated 130,000 copies, and a smartly remixed version of "Nappy Heads," emphasizing a live sound, proved a fairly potent single on the dance-track circuit, as did another remix of the already crisp "Vocab." But even this success was shot down by the constant critical nods to the fact that Lauryn and her singing, in particular on the sweet, soulful song "Some Seek Stardom," were the best things about the album and that she would be wise to leave the group and go solo.

Lauryn took those statements as backhanded compliments and continued to mouth the group watchwords, "family" and "triad," in defense of the knocks against Wyclef and Pras. "You had the people who always thought I was with the wrong crew," she said to *Vibe*. "There was always a lot of energy for me to do something solo but, to me, it was a little bit negative. It was flattering, but it was like 'Cross them cats; get rid of them.' But that's not me. I'm not a jump ship type of person."

Lauryn, admittedly young and naive in the face of those comments making her out to be the whole show, chose largely to ignore the critics in the hope that they would eventually go away. And while the constant call for her to go solo did eventually calm down, it had, indeed, dealt the group a blow that it would never completely recover from.

She felt those comments were painful and they did cause some strain in the group. Lauryn felt the comments were forcing her brothers in music to feel she might soon leave the group.

In the meantime, Lauryn, Pras and Wyclef got together and picked through the remains of the promising but, to their way of thinking, flawed *Blunted on Reality*. They realized that the inconsistency of their sound was the result of too many producers not in tune with what they were trying to say. So the first thing they did was go back to their management and record company and tell them they wanted out of their original production contract and that, from now on, the only one who would produce the Fugees would be the Fugees—assuming there would be another record.

Columbia Records, with their eye always on the bottom line, had not been thrilled with the sales of *Blunted on Reality*. The promotion budget for the record was slashed to nothing and there was serious talk in the corporate tower, due in part to the group's recent bad-mouthing of the recording of *Blunted on Reality*, of jettisoning the group as well. Ruffhouse, however, despite feeling a bit disappointed by the Fugees's shots at the producers of the album, truly believed in the trio, and they hung tough. They scraped together their limited resources to continue to get the word out on the group and took an old school approach by encouraging the group to make another record—their kind of record.

"Any place else and we would have been dropped," offered Lauryn, giving props to their label, in the *Philadelphia Inquirer*. "But Ruffhouse convinced us that there was a future."

Wyclef ultimately predicted in *Vibe* that the second time around would be the charm for the Fugees: "The production on our last album was wack. But with the next album, we're not working with the same people. Our next album is going to be the bomb."

Early in 1995, the group prepared for what they considered their make-or-break album by setting up a studio in East Orange, New Jersey, called the Booga Basement. Inside the freshly painted, newly equipped walls, the trio found a sense of freedom from outside influences. Here, they reasoned, they could do "their thing."

Slowly but surely, the new music began to come together. To the casual visitor, the new music sounded like one long song broken up by techno echoes, upbeat jazz riffs and Lauryn's looping, often lighter-than-air singing. But repeated listenings began to show distinct personalities beginning to emerge within the grooves.

"Fu-Gee-La," which the Fugees were already jokingly referring to as their first hit single, had a lighter-than-air, soulful quality. The decision to remake Roberta Flack's "Killing Me Softly with His Song" turned out to be the right one when Lauryn's alternately soulful and seductive singing provided an amazing odyssey through the electronic-instrumental wizardry of Pras and Wyclef. There was also tough stuff, message songs like "Beast" and "Zealots"—righteous, angry tunes that showed that the Fugees were not lightweight and that they could get down in the street and rumble smartly with the gangsta rappers.

Lauryn was continuing her studies at Columbia University but was having a hard time keeping her mind on her education when the music was always in her thoughts. In her spare time, she found herself scribbling lyrics, experimenting with vocal inflections and basically thinking about the next session in the Booga Basement. It was during this period that Lauryn, for the first time, did some session work when she added her particular brand of soul to one of the cuts on crooner D'Angelo's 1995 recording, *Brown Sugar*. In 1995, Lauryn was also tempted to get back into acting when an offer came for her to play a role in the movie bio pic about the Black Panthers called *Panther*. Lauryn, however, felt that rescheduling the Fugees's planned studio date to do a movie was not right, so she declined.

But the next Fugees album remained uppermost in everybody's mind. Wyclef, who had been particularly upset with the reception *Blunted on Reality* had received, was wildly optimistic as the collection of eclectic sounds and words came together. "We decided we weren't going to let anyone limit us by telling us we couldn't do something, he reported in *Rolling Stone*. "If I wanted a real jungle vibe or a Pink Floyd vibe, I was going to do it."

However, the very freedom that was making for creative electricity during sessions was also heating up the personal and professional relationship between Lauryn and Wyclef. The friendly competition between the pair on *Blunted on Reality* had kicked up a notch and the competition for the best lyric and the best rhyme would occasionally turn angry during the sessions for the new album.

Wyclef, however, was generous in giving Lauryn her props for her contributions to the album in postrecording interviews. To his way of thinking, the entire concept and format of the album was Lauryn's idea. "She was like, 'It would be ill if we did this cinematic, but audio so the people who are listening to the album, you can take them on an ear ride versus a visual ride,' " he reported in the FC Grove Web Site. "And like Lauryn really captured the Roberta Flack soul."

Then there were those days in the studio when, according to Pras, being in the Fugees was the only thing that stood between the members of the group and the grind of the real world. The day they did the song "Ready or Not," the three of them were each going through some personal pain. Lauryn was crying when she did her vocals. He marveled to see her singing with tears coming out of her eyes.

Lauryn, on many occasions, was downright aggressive in demanding that a song go her way, and the skirmishes would often get ugly. The members of the Fugees all had to agree, however, that the competition was good for the music. For Lauryn it was yet another reminder that the only way to get her way was to go solo. And while part of her was ready to break away, there was an almost fanatical sense of personal and creative loyalty to the group that was holding her back. "At the time I was quite content singing Fugees's songs," she declared in *Ebony*. Yet those close to Lauryn knew that that was not entirely the case.

The new album was completed shortly before Thanksgiving in 1995. The mastered tape was taken over to Columbia-Ruffhouse where the bigwigs listened and smiled broadly. From a corporate point of view there seemed to be enough singles. But the smiles froze when they heard the jazz and the other elements that did not fall into a nice, neat, commercial package. Their minds flashed on "hard sell."

The Fugees, however, felt differently. "Somewhere on this planet, the album will win," predicted Wyclef in *Vibe*, "because the music that we're doing, we're doing it for the people.''

The new album would be called *The Score*. The group liked the idea behind the title, because they felt it was time to settle the score (with critics and music lovers). Lauryn Hill sat back and smiled. Getting even sounded good to her.

What's the Score?

The buzz on *The Score* began early in 1996.

In order to give the fans a taste of things to come, the Fugees decided to release the single "Fu-Gee-La" in advance of the album. The record company thought so much of the buzz surrounding *The Score* that they willingly coughed up a decent budget for a "Fu-Gee-La" video that had the crew running from thugs in the streets and in the jungles of Jamaica. The Fugees were not in the country long, but Lauryn formed an immediate emotional and spiritual tie with the land that had spawned Bob Marley and the sound of reggae.

Prereleasing the single and video turned out to be a stroke of genius. Radio programmers were all over the song, immediately adding it to their playlists. MTV loved the song and accompanying video, so much so that it was immediately put into the coveted "heavy rotation" slot. The single was already certified gold when the Fugees dropped *The Score* early in February 1996. The album entered the influential *Billboard* charts at number twelve that first week and would sell an amazing total of two hundred thousand albums a week well into March. *The Score* was hanging in at the top of the charts, rather than quickly fading like most rap records had up to that point. That fact and the sheer musical diversity of the album was not lost on the critics, both black and white, who were lining up to proclaim *The Score* one of the top ten records of the year, only three months into the year.

The magazine *Rap Pages* loudly praised the album by stating, "The Fugees have succeeded in creating one of the most innovative rap albums in recent memory." *Rolling Stone* exclaimed, "The Fugees are a Neapolitan treat, sweet in three layers: rhyme, sample and groove." *Q* magazine crowed, "The album is an impressively, panoramic soundscape." *Entertainment Weekly* continued the accolades by stating in a four-star review that "*The Score* feels warm and intimate because the Fugees sound so relaxed and natural."

The unprecedented success of *The Score* was a happy surprise, especially to Lauryn who, based on the sales of *Blunted on Reality*, had suspected that this album would do nothing more than continue their slow but steady climb to the top. "I'm surprised at the speed with which it took off," she said in *Phoenix New Times*. "We thought we'd have an underground success and that it would take a minute for people to realize what it was."

The group's attempt to connect with the streets, utilizing a raw-hard mixture of funk, hip-hop, jazz, reggae and doo-wop elements, had worked. Lauryn laughingly categorized *The Score* as a little rice and beans, mixed with a little collard greens, a little mango and watermelon. The truth was nobody in the Fugees had any idea that the record was going to do as well as it did.

Lauryn, however, had a theory that led straight back to the hood. "We wanted to make music for the kids that grew up like us," she said in *Rolling Stone*. "Some people might think 'Well, they play instruments so we can make this group more accessible to white folks.' But we're not going for that alternative label. All we're trying to do is bring back a musicality, a raw essence that's been lost."

The Score immediately hit the streets and, true to Lauryn's prediction, opened the eyes of young urban music lovers to the possibilities of hip-hop beyond the cliches of bad language and gangsta themes.

To be sure, there was some backlash in the rap world against *The Score*. The hard-core community laughed at what they termed the "lightweight approach" of the Fugees's music. Brooklyn rapper Jeru the Damaja took some shots at the group in *Trip* magazine when he called their cover of "Killing Me Softly" "fake-ass R & B" and termed their reworking of some of the lyrics of the Bob Marley classic "No Woman No Cry" as "blasphemy."

Even Hill's mother came face-to-face with preconceptions about what rap and hip-hop should be. "A teacher I worked with confronted me once and said 'I know how you raised your kids. How is it that your daughter can relate to ghetto kids?' " recalled Valerie Hill in *Spin*. "And I was quite taken aback. I told her that Lauryn relates because of her humanity. She's not limited to people who were raised like her."

It was at this point that Lauryn made the decision to drop out of Columbia University midway through her sophomore year. There were tons of press interviews to wade through and a big-time tour of the United States and Canada was being set up. Formal education would have to go on hold. But her real-world education was about to begin.

The Fugees's first major tour was a bus odyssey through the United States and Canada into places like Montreal's Club Metropolis, Toronto's Phoenix Concert Theater and a ton of venues in places like Chi Town and the Motor City. It was a typical tour in so many ways. But for the Fugees it was all exciting and new.

The sound system at the clubs and concert halls was not always the best, security would often deny them access to their own show and there was a myriad of minor squabbles with their opening acts. In between gigs, interview sessions, signing autographs, dealing with such business as turning down a Sprite commercial offer and complaints about who gets the bunk over the bus engine, the Fugees solidified as a family. They ate together, braided each other's hair and bitched about and at each other. But mostly it was learning that they could do this and not split apart, despite the fact that there were already forces at work trying to do just that.

Once again the media push was that Lauryn was the whole show and that it was only a matter of time before she left the group and the guys in the dust. Pras, who had already had it up to here with that, took a moment during the Canadian portion of the tour to address the issue one more time. "The whole industry was saying that," said the exasperated musician in *Vibe*. "But there will be no breaking up. Lauryn won't chow down unless Clef's being served, too. Blood runs thicker than loot in the Fugee clique. We can't stop being cousins."

For her part, Lauryn continued to deny that there was dissension in the ranks, preferring to offer that the role of hip-hop women, based on what was happening with performers like herself, was changing from the superficial to the realistic. "If you look good and you rhyme, you get that much more props," she told a *Vibe* reporter. "If I had one eye lower than the other, I probably wouldn't be as dope as everyone claims I am. I keep my clothes on so I'm not emphasizing that part of me." Lauryn also raged at the negative images projected by female rappers and predicted dire consequences.

Lauryn had always maintained a fairly active social life but was rarely seen out in public with anybody except Pras and Wyclef and their requisite posse; which continued to raise the rumor that she was, in fact, having an affair with one or, as the more outlandish falsehoods speculated, both of her bandmates. There were also lurid, tabloid-style tales that Lauryn, in fact, did not like men at all. These lies were usually laughed at by Lauryn and the boys and promptly forgotten. The truth was much easier to deal with and the truth was that Lauryn had never found the time, inclination or the right person to get deeply involved in a romantic relationship.

That attitude had not changed, but with the elevation of the Fugees to superstar status she was suddenly finding herself the object of a lot of men's affections. And Lauryn, now twenty, was finding that she liked the attention. She began dating—men within the industry and out. But Lauryn had a penchant for secrecy regarding her private life especially the romantic aspect of her life. The reason is that Lauryn had been hiding a heartbreak that had left her wounded and tentative in love.

Who the man was remains a mystery to this day. Lauryn has never named names, which once again fanned the flames of a rumored bad relationship with Wyclef. But reading between the lines, the mysterious relationship seems to have been intense. And like many such affairs, it had its ups and downs. But Lauryn, in a rare moment of candor in *Essence*, regarding her lost love, made it plain that she had tried her damnedest to make it work.

"I'd spent so many years working at a relationship that didn't work that I was just like 'I'm going to write these songs and pour my heart into them.'"

Lauryn has rarely acknowledged that relationship and, when she has, it has been in the context of a betrayal to her own moral and religious upbringing. "What I did was one of the biggest sins you can do when you have such a tight relationship with God," she confessed to *Essence*, midway through the U.S. portion of the Fugees's 1996 tour.

"I put someone before Him. I fell deeply in love and put a man before God."

On the other hand, Lauryn seemed quite in control of her emotions when it came to dealing with the media demands brought on by the fact that *The Score*, by the time the Fugees hit the road in early 1996, had already been certified multiplatinum and was being touted as the first album in a long time to approach 20 million in sales. The press seemed to appreciate her candor in describing the group's rise to the top and they delighted in the way this soft-spoken woman could catch fire if the question happened to touch a nerve.

That Lauryn was morally straight and religious—in direct contrast to the street personnas usually offered up by rappers—as well as attractive made her the one that the press usually sought out. Lauryn felt that because she was one female surrounded by guys, she got the lion's share of the attention.

But in reality, especially after "Killing Me Softly" was released as the follow-up single and radio programmers began playing more of the cuts on *The Score*, Lauryn as a singer and producer was beginning once again to stand out as the Fugees's centerpiece. However, Lauryn recollected in *Vibe* that even in the heyday of *The Score*'s climb up the charts, convincing the public that she was more than a pretty face with a velvet tongue was still an uphill battle. She commented, "I think part of it had to do with the fact that I was with a group of guys who were perceived as being the breath and the life and the reason I do what I do. I was also an individual as much as I was a part of the group but, because I championed the group so strongly, they thought I had no legs to stand on."

Life on the road quickly went from the excitement of performing in front of a new audience in a different town each night to the monotony of faceless hotel rooms, restaurants and arenas. There was little time for anything except the perfunctory after-show party, at which Lauryn tended to make only token appearances, and the onslaught of the media that wanted to know everything and anything but inevitably ended up asking the same dozen questions over and over again. The Fugees began to live for the two hours they were on stage each night and learned to live with the other twenty-two.

"We stayed on tour for a long time," reflected Lauryn of the grind in *Vibe*. "Tour is interesting because it ain't home, which means it's not reality. It's the road. Every night you play for an audience that's clapping for what you do, so you have this warped sense of self."

Unfortunately for Lauryn, the isolation and boredom of the road only served to magnify the frustration she felt over the lack of romance in her life and the insensitivity of the men she had been meeting over the years.

"Right now I'm a lot hurt and a lot disappointed," she confessed to *Essence* forty-two days into the '96 U.S. tour and after a successful two-night stand at Los Angeles's famed House of Blues. "Half of the niggas that I meet, they don't know about relationships. And when they hurt you, they don't know it. Or, if they do know, they don't really give a f—— because they've been so bruised, battered and scarred themselves."

This was also the period in which Lauryn, whose continued rumored love relationship with Wyclef was beginning to sound more and more like the real thing, admitted to suffering a lack of faith: "The reason why I stopped praying was because there was some things in my life that I knew weren't good for me," she confessed in *Rolling Stone*. "But I decided that I needed those things and that, if I prayed, God would take them from me."

Lauryn's inner thoughts continued to be in torment. Her personal life was out of control. But fate was about to intervene and she would not be alone for much longer.

The Fugees had just finished another emotionally draining show and walked off to thunderous

applause from yet another appreciative audience.
Lauryn smiled a tired smile as she prepared for the
after-show ritual of meeting and greeting the local
record reps, disc jockeys and promoters. Of course,
there were the usual groupies and hangers-on to
contend with—and as she stood in the middle of a
crowd, one of them was coming her way.

Rohan Marley had quietly made headlines on
two fronts. First as one of the many offspring of
reggae legend Bob Marley and later as a standout
football player on the University of Miami team
and the Ottawa Roughriders in the Canadian Football League. At first glance he did not have "stud"
written all over him. Rohan was stocky rather than
lean—stocky in a muscular way. His features and
piercing, contented eyes contrasted wildly with the
typical bland Hollywood types. The impression
was that he was not classically good-looking, but
rather interesting in a rugged sort of way. Lauryn's
initial impression was that if he was on the make
she would at least be subjected to a different line.

Consequently she was not surprised that he carried himself with an air of confidence as he moved
through the after-show crowd. And so, amid the
superficial, schmoozing nature of this after-show
get-together, Rohan was at the top of his game as
he glided smooth as silk over to Lauryn.

He said hi and immediately began talking her

up, complimenting her on the way she moved on-stage and the way she held her guitar. Lauryn smiled politely and returned the small talk. In her mind she was thinking "this is a good-looking man." But she also knew that this was part of the game and she had played this game many times before and lost.

"He said 'Hey!' " laughed Lauryn at the memory of that first meeting in an *Essence* interview. " 'Hey, I like you. I want to talk to you.' But back then I really wasn't into checking for anybody."

But Rohan persisted. And Lauryn had to admit that there was a certain amount of sincerity coming through the confident exterior. Which was why, at the end of the evening, she willingly exchanged telephone numbers with him. Lauryn, as she left the arena, was in a sudden emotional quandary. Part of her hoped he would never use that number. Part of her hoped he would.

Rohan did call and, during the rare breaks in the Fugees's 1996 tour, they began to hook up. It was nothing heavy at first: long walks, long talks and the occasional movie. It was in this relaxed atmosphere that Lauryn found herself drawn to Rohan's very human qualities. He was consistent in his thoughts and attitudes. He was as good as his word. Lauryn knew that Rohan was not in awe of the star-making machine and Lauryn's celebrity, a fact that allowed her to open up to him and share her innermost thoughts. She was comfortable around him. Most importantly, given Lauryn's emotional state of mind at the time, he was there and available. She began calling him by a pet name—Ro. It was not long before Lauryn admitted to herself that she was in love with this quiet man with the legendary last name.

She felt Rohan was the first guy who actually took care of her. Lauryn likened the feeling to that of a lion protecting its young.

And so, as the Fugees tour continued through the United States and then Europe, Lauryn and Rohan made the time to fall in love—in secret. The couple were in agreement that they did not want their relationship played out in the media, so they took great pains to keep it quiet. This only added fuel to the mystery of a lack of a man in Lauryn's life. Lauryn laughed at the big deal that was being made of her personal life but acknowledged that she could see how the perception of her as a lonely woman could be made. She acknowledged that people had never seen her with a man in public and so it wasn't too hard to see how the press would think that she was alone.

Building a relationship with Rohan was going to be a challenge. But as the days and weeks went by she was finding him to be the perfect emotional and spiritual match. He was not big on wild displays of emotion, especially in public, and so Lauryn was thrilled when he did the little things—putting his hand gently on her arm and snuggling close so that Lauryn could put her head on his broad shoulder for support—so well. This man who came so suddenly into her life caused Lauryn to rethink her attitudes toward being with a man in this business.

"He came to me when I wasn't looking for anybody," she reflected in a 1998 *Los Angeles Times* conversation. "I'd never met anyone like him. Ro is not frightened by my success. He doesn't feel the need to be competitive. And I wasn't used to that at first. I was like, 'What's wrong with you?' I'd try to pick fights with him. But with Ro it was just pure love."

During this period, Lauryn Hill was also doing what she could do to help other people. The singer had always been keen on giving back to the community. Shortly before the release of *The Score*, Lauryn came up with the idea of a day camp for inner-city children that would keep youngsters off the street and out of trouble. To fund this idea, she conceived of the Refugee Project, an outreach organization designed to generate funds to get her dream up and running. The scope of the Refugee Project soon expanded to raise money for orphans and Haitian refugees who had been sent home by the United States government.

During the May 1996 leg in the Fugees's tour, Lauryn had another idea. Always a big proponent of the power of the vote, Lauryn, while the Fugees were wowing audiences on the Continent, came up with a plan to boost voter registration in the minority community by staging a series of free concerts in New York, Newark and Miami which would go under the banner of Hoodshock. Lauryn's timetable for the shows was short and was not realistic, either logistically or economically.

But Lauryn was determined to make Hoodshock happen immediately. From a phone in her hotel room, somewhere in Europe, Lauryn rang up every record-company executive she knew, stated her case and then asked for money. Lots of money. In less than a month she managed to raise two hundred thousand dollars as seed money for the concerts. Now all she needed was some of the biggest acts in rap and hip-hop to agree to play for free and for a good cause. While not always the hallmark of hard-core performers, the likes of Sean "Puffy" Combs, Wu-Tang Clan, Biggie Smalls and Doug E. Fresh jumped at Lauryn's request and a series of shows, to include appearances by the Fugees, were quickly put together.

Unfortunately Lauryn's charitable good works ran afoul of a man with a gun at the first show, held in New York, resulting in a stampede and thirty injuries. In short order, the remaining shows were canceled. Lauryn, while disappointed, remained upbeat at what she perceived as a success on a social level: "The way I look at it, the event was a huge success," she assured *Rolling Stone*. "All we wanted to do was help the kids and the community."

Midway through 1996, Lauryn took a tentative first step in the direction of solo work when she recorded the ballad "The Sweetest Thing" for the *Love Jones* movie soundtrack. It was only her second musical outing without Wyclef or Pras in the picture and it was, at first, strange to be working with other musicians. It was also unusual for her to be producing the cut as well. But Lauryn was determined to make the most of it.

"When I went to the bridge on 'The Sweetest Thing' I wanted changes and people were like 'What the hell is that?' " she related in *Vibe*. "I said, 'It's a change. Remember?' They used to have those in songs back in the day."

The foray into this relatively minor outside project fueled the ongoing media speculation that Lauryn had outgrown the Fugees and was about to go solo. She once again attempted to put that rumor to rest by stating she was very content doing songs with the Fugees.

The latter stages of the Fugees's U.S. tour and

the early portion of the European tour was beginning to exact a physical toll on Lauryn. As the Fugees's tour raced through the Christmas season, she was physically exhausted much of the time and was finding herself mentally scattered and occasionally would find it difficult to concentrate onstage.

It was only as an afterthought that she realized she had missed her period. A trip to the doctor confirmed her suspicion. The twenty-one-year-old singer was pregnant.

Lauryn immediately contacted Rohan. She was not sure how he was going to take the news and what the news would do to their relationship. And while he was just as shocked as Lauryn was, she was thrilled when he told her that he was there for her and their baby. Her parents took the news with equal parts of excitement and relief, the latter because Rohan would be there and so their daughter was not going to end up being a mother alone. And finally she told Pras and Wyclef. Lauryn's bandmates knew that Rohan had been in the picture for quite some time and, in their dealings with him, had given the relationship their unofficial blessing. However, the look on their faces said that their singer getting pregnant had not been in their game plan. But their hugs and words of support also told Lauryn that everything in their professional lives would work out.

And working out meant that the Fugees would continue to tour until Lauryn could not tour anymore, and that her pregnancy would be kept top secret. The tour continued with Lauryn, now regularly dressed in baggy clothing to hide what she perceived as her growing belly, continuing to hold up her end of the bargain by providing the trademark exotic, progressive vocals and larger-than-life presence that, despite the group dynamic, had put the Fugees on the map.

Lauryn onstage was the same dynamic performer, moving with a renewed sense of style and grace and putting even more emotion into her singing. Offstage she had begun to curtail the postconcert partying and would typically go straight to her room and go to sleep.

However, despite her best efforts, rumors eventually began to surface that Lauryn was, in fact, pregnant and, more and more, her media interviews inevitably turned into an inquisition in which the question of whether she was pregnant and who the father was became the overriding issue. Lauryn did her best to deny the fact good-naturedly but, as the questions continued to come, her resolve and her patience began to cave in. Finally, early in 1997, when the lethargy and morning sickness had become a daily part of Lauryn's life, she lost it.

Lauryn was being interviewed by the notorious gossip jock Wendy Williams and was being pressed on the pregnancy issue. Finally, in tones both defiant and silky-smooth, she told the interviewer, "I know this is your job, but this is my life." The remark seemingly put Williams in her place and the interview drew to a close. But the effect of the interview and the seemingly constant assault on her personal life was taking its toll.

"I was in the woman's face and there was no compassion," she sighed in the aftermath of the Williams interview in *Vibe*. "I was twenty-one years old and I was happy and confused at the same time. I was trying to figure out what to do with my life. But, because I was young and successful, that made my personal life something for everybody to know."

Lauryn's hormone-fed confusion was also being tested by the very people in whom she had confided her secret. Close friends were telling her, in subtle and not so subtle ways, that maybe she should not have the baby and that it was not too late to have an abortion.

"A lot of people said 'Girl, you've got a career, it's not the right time; you're a superstar. Don't be having no baby now,' " she sadly recalled in *Essence* of the pressures put on her. "I had a conversation with Nina Simone and she said 'Lauryn,

I don't think that a woman can have a baby and be in the music business.' I thought 'Okay, this is a hard one,' and so I prayed on it. I knew God was never going to give me a sign not to be pregnant. At least it didn't for me.''

In looking at her life up to that point, Lauryn found a lot that made her decision to have this child a lot easier. She was financially in good shape, she had a man in her life who loved her and she had a supportive family. She felt she would be a good mother and that the only reason not to have this child was that it would inconvenience her career. And that was not a good enough excuse not to have the baby.''

The Fugees continued to tour into the new year but with Lauryn now in her early weeks of pregnancy, it was evident that the tour would shortly be coming to an end. The group managed another four weeks of touring. By this time Lauryn's pregnancy was the worst-kept secret on the planet and so it made ending the tour in her second month much easier to do. Lauryn returned home, with the rumors now being replaced by even more confusing half-truths. One of the most laughable news items named Stephen Marley, another of Bob Marley's many sons, as the father of Lauryn's baby.

Lauryn continued to play the game. She jokingly

continued to deny that she was pregnant despite the fact that her belly was beginning to bulge noticeably beneath her stylish clothes. And when it came to the question of the father, the expectant mother was equally mum. Rohan was obviously in Lauryn's life at this point and was, in many quarters, considered the prime suspect in the fatherhood question. Rohan's comments on their relationship were equally vague. He would only acknowledge that "she's my queen."

Family, friends and, most importantly, the music industry felt that the saga of Lauryn Hill was about to end or, at the very least, go on hiatus: especially when there was no inclination on Lauryn's part to help Pras out on his solo album *Ghetto Supastar*. People thought she would most certainly take two years off, the Fugees would go into a tailspin and most certainly dissolve and motherhood would either blunt or totally destroy her ability to be a creative force.

Lauryn Hill felt differently. She felt she was right on track, both emotionally and creatively.

So much so that Lauryn changed her mind about participating in solo projects when Wyclef announced he was going into the studio to do a solo album called *The Carnival* by a loosely aligned group of musician friends and influences called the Refugee All-Stars. Lauryn immediately joined with

Pras to contribute to Wyclef's cause. It was a relaxed time for Lauryn. This was Wyclef's thing and she was comfortable just being one of the tools with which he would create his magic. In typical Wyclef manner, *The Carnival* was a sea of influences—everything from pop to hip-hop to reggae to classical and all points in-between. Wyclef moved Lauryn through the paces, allowing her freedom to play in different musical playgrounds and opening her eyes to even more diverse musical possibilities that might soon become a part of her world.

Amazingly, Lauryn's pregnancy signaled a very creative time for all three members of the Fugees. Their activity away from each other and in different musical venues shored up the fact that Wyclef, Pras and Lauryn were their own people and, contrary to their fans' desires, the Fugees would not be the beginning and the end of their creative life.

"It's a blessing that we have the opportunity to do separate musical endeavors," proclaimed Lauryn in *Vibe* in the wake of her work on *The Carnival*. "All of us have the need to entertain, so that is why you see us out there doing other things that don't involve the other two."

Pras agreed with Lauryn's assessment of their rugged individuality. "If it's the Fugees then we have to compromise. With the Fugees you get the flavor of all three. When we go solo, it's our own thing.''

For Lauryn, guesting on Wyclef's album was also a break from the negative vibes and intrusions that continued to make her life a road of endless bumps and dips—elements that would reenter her life with the completion of her work on *The Carnival*. Suggestions both personal and professional would continue to hover around Lauryn.

Lauryn, who was never at a loss for an opinion but was always willing to argue and finesse to get her way, found herself growing more outspoken and militant as she continued to explore her creative world. As *The Score* was reaching the 14-million-records-sold level and the Fugees landed a pair of Grammy nominations, she was finding it sadly ironic that the group's music, which she felt had pushed the envelope of political and social awareness in the black community, was being bought largely by middle-class whites who, she believed, did not have a clue about the reality of what they had been singing about and were into the Fugees because interest in the band had suddenly become hip.

She also found herself taking exception to the rare knocks against the album and, in particular, the song ''Killing Me Softly,'' which, more than one critic intoned, would soon be in the repertoire

of every wedding band on the planet. Admittedly
it was more a tongue-in-cheek remark than a vi-
cious attack but Lauryn, in a constantly defensive
state of mind, took the comments as showing a lack
of respect.

Consequently Lauryn was in a testy mood on the
night of the Grammy Awards in February 1997. It
had not been very long since she had seen Pras and
Wyclef but there was a renewed sense of excitement and anticipation as the trio traded hugs, kisses
and news prior to the Grammy ceremony. For the
moment Lauryn, dressed to the nines in stylish
clothes, was at ease.

But her ire rose again, later in the evening,
when the Fugees stepped onstage to accept their
awards for Best Rap Album and Best R & B Album by a Duo or Group. In thinly veiled comments during the band's acceptance speech and
later in post-Grammy comments to MTV and
members of the press, Lauryn expressed her
views about what she felt were the faults of the
music industry and many of the groups they
spawned, and also indicated, controversially, that
she hoped that only black people would buy the
Fugees's albums. The flames were fanned again
when, during an interview on the notorious How-
ard Stern Show, an anonymous caller called in to
say that Lauryn had recently told an interviewer,

"I would rather see babies starve than have white people buy Fugees's records."

Word spread like wildfire about Lauryn's "racist" remarks. Pras and Wyclef, who were more than a bit mystified themselves by Lauryn's comments, did their best to mollify the growing backlash against the group by saying that Lauryn was not racist and that the Fugees's music was for all people. Lauryn would backtrack in subsequent interviews, stating that what she had said was misinterpreted. However, she never reneged on her earlier statements that she thought real music was losing out to shallow hype and marketing plans.

"Some asshole obviously twisted what I said because he was threatened by it," she said defensively of the Stern call in *Spin*. "I don't have hate for anybody. I grew up with everybody."

For their part, the Fugees's management and record company ducked for cover. They were not happy with Lauryn's remarks but, like everyone else, they realized she was already too powerful a force in the music business to cross. If anything, Lauryn's diatribe seemed to have the opposite effect. Record sales continued to soar and the controversy eventually went away.

The Fugees always seemed to be informed about what was happening in Haiti, and what they found was not a pretty picture. High unemployment, poverty and a growing incidence of AIDS among the populace had given the country a terrible reputation around the world. In an attempt to foster self-pride in the people of Haiti as well as to raise much-needed money for local charities, the group decided to put on a concert in Haiti, the first ever headlined by a popular American group.

Word spread like wildfire that the Fugees were coming to town and, by the time the April 13, 1997, concert date rolled around, more than seventy thousand people had crowded into an area of the Port-au-Prince waterfront. The group was energized by the prospect of playing in front of their people. Their enthusiasm showed in an extravaganza of sights and sounds. Wyclef and Pras were all over the stage, throwing themselves into exaggerated gyrations and laying down monster passages of ethnically pure yet progressive music. Lauryn, likewise, felt very much in the moment, her voice alternating between tough raps and soothing trebles and scats.

The concert, which also featured a number of local acts, was not only a successful event but also opened Lauryn's eyes to some of the contrasts in the world. She had found Haiti to be a lush, exotic, peaceful place. Unfortunately the idyllic vision was often punctuated by jarring scenes of poverty and disease. They were images that would forever be embedded in her mind.

And they were images that were magnified a thousandfold every time she felt a kick in her belly.

SIX

Miseducation

Lauryn was euphoric as the car taking her to the Detroit airport rounded smoothly onto the turnpike heading out of town—euphoric at the prospect of impending motherhood, and positively ecstatic at having passed her first major hurdle as songwriter and producer for no less a personality than Aretha Franklin.

She had been apprehensive on a number of fronts. The song she had penned for Lady Soul, ''A Rose Is Still a Rose,'' was written in a very hip-hop way, full of '90s rhythm and attitude, and she knew Aretha was nothing if not very old school. And then there was the question of musicianship and bringing a rough-and-ready instrumental sound to the normally glossy, heavily orchestrated Franklin sound. But Lauryn was determined to stand her ground in the studio.

"When I wrote the song [for Aretha], the rhythm, the syncopation was definitely hip-hop," she explained in *Spin*. "I expected to have to really go through it with her. But she took the demo version of the song, came in the studio and it was done."

Lauryn was so caught up in the musical moment that, on a whim, she instructed her driver to take a swing through town and stop at the famed Motown Museum. Wandering through the halls and gazing at memorabilia immortalizing such stars as Stevie Wonder, the Supremes and the Jackson Five had a mesmerizing effect on her. "It was incredible to me and really inspiring," she reflected in *Time* of her walk through soul history.

Lauryn left the museum determined to go solo. But she had one more professional stop to make on the road to motherhood—the recording of her song "On That Day" by CeCe Winans. She was overjoyed as she remembered that session: "We were in the studio together, singing and dancing."

In the middle of it, Lauryn suddenly started feeling a little funny. Instinctively she knew that she was about to go into labor. On the day "my little man showed up" the hospital delivery room was a virtual United Nations that included her mother, a Senegalese assistant, a Jamaican midwife and a Jewish obstetrician. Lauryn remembered in an *Essence* interview how hilarious it all was the day Zion came into the world on August 3, 1997: "My doctor had this really strong accent and the midwife had a West African–French accent. So my mother was like 'Girl push! C'mon girl, push!' And the assistant was like 'Push dahling! Oh push dahling!' And the midwife was like 'Push gal! Yuh ha fi push it out!' And the doctor was totally nonchalant like 'Oh push, push, push.' It was hilarious."

The next eight months were a flurry of personal bliss and professional growth. Lauryn had returned to her South Orange, New Jersey, home where she spent almost every waking hour attending to the needs of her newborn son. She recalled being totally refocused by Zion. That he became the sole focus of her days and nights was a marvel to her.

Lauryn was adamant about not disclosing the name of the father of her child. Even eight months after the birth, amid continued speculation that Rohan, a frequent visitor to the house, was the father, Lauryn continued to deny all rumors: "I felt like the world had enough of me. I felt like I put my soul on records and I didn't have to answer any global question about who my boyfriend was."

With the Fugees on hiatus, it was inevitable that the boys in the band would use the time off to turn their attention to outside opportunities. Pras had watched as *Ghetto Supastar* was released to solid reviews and sales. Wyclef, likewise, was already watching as the release of *The Carnival*, garnered reviews that showed that he was a true power behind the Fugees's throne. The news that Pras and Wyclef were, like Lauryn, already beginning to field outside offers only served to fan Lauryn's creative flames.

Every free moment found Lauryn with pencil and paper writing snatches of lyrics and rhymes that would eventually become songs—deeply personal songs that, despite her current happiness, often hearkened back to the "dysfunctional" relationships and darker days of her life as well as the expected songs that centered around happiness and motherhood.

"It's more about me finding myself," Lauryn told *Rolling Stone* when stating her goals in songwriting. "I'm not embarrassed to expose myself in the sense that I'm human. I'm not embarrassed to tell someone how happy I was when I had my child, or how conflicted I was or how much I love God."

However there was more to her aspirations than exploring her soul. Lauryn was, before all else, a fan of music, and with the opportunity "to sit still once I had my child" she was, these days, finding little inspiration in the areas of rap and hip-hop coming out of the music industry's machine. What she was finding was a materialistic approach to creating urban music in which talent and musical skills were taking a backseat to marketing and hype.

She complained that the MCs didn't have to write their rhymes and the singers didn't really have to be able to sing. For Lauryn it just felt like the world of music had just been turned upside down.

Lauryn was contemplating a utopian musical world where talented musicians and songwriters created real flesh-and-blood music. And she was contemplating being the center of this new world. Once again she insisted to an *Ebony* reporter that it had to be real: "To write something that's too pretentious, that wouldn't feel natural to me. Once you release something, it's a reflection of you and people [if they don't like it] will beat it up. So I knew I'd better do what I had to do to put my best foot forward."

By the time the Fugees had stepped onstage to receive their Grammys for *The Score*, Lauryn's plans for her solo album had begun to solidify. She had the songs. And she was already making plans to populate her album with live musicians. She was contemplating a wish list of favorite superstar performers who, she fantasized, would fly in from all over the world to lay down a simple lick or sing a single line. However, the little-girl dreams soon dissolved into a determined sense of grown-up reality. Which meant turning to the hood and the brothers who she felt knew the score.

From nearby Newark, Lauryn landed the hot, local players Vada Nobles, Johari Newton, Tejumold Newton and Rasheem Pugh. Ché Guevara, a hot young re-mixer who had spiced up the work of Destiny's Child and Wyclef's solo project, was like a little kid when Lauryn rang him up and asked him to help her out. "All I could think of was that I was going to be working with one of my idols," said Guevara, to Sonic Net, "and I really had to work hard to keep my cool."

Finally Lauryn called up one of the topflight engineers in the business, Gordon Williams, to sit at her elbow throughout the sessions. This last choice would ultimately turn out to be the most important one because Lauryn, in her quiet moments, was seriously thinking about producing the album herself. She had already produced two tracks for two distinguished singers and a soundtrack cut that had been well received. But a whole album, populated by veteran players, was a whole different ball game. Could she handle all that and a baby, too?

Once it became official that Lauryn was preparing to go into the studio to record her first solo album, the consensus around town was that she would need help—lots of it. The rumor mill began spitting out a number of potential producers. The two most often mentioned were Wyclef and RZA from the Wu-Tang Clan. Lauryn had a good laugh at the names being floated. In her mind she had already made her choice.

"The album was becoming so personal," she related in *Rolling Stone*. "I knew I had to do it myself. I guess people figure producing is something that women don't really know about. But I was already a legitimate producer [coexecutive producer on *The Score*]. It's just that my name was totally ignored because it was beside a man's."

And not just any man's. Lauryn's fame and fortune, as well as her personal life, had been linked with Wyclef by the media since the beginning. It is not surprising that she wanted to run the whole show on her first solo album. It was surprising, however, that she would not even extend an offer to Wyclef and Pras even to sit in on a cut or two.

Lauryn sensed that this perceived slight would ultimately make for some hard feelings and could be the last nail in the coffin of what many were already signaling as the demise of the Fugees. But she was not about to knuckle under to any pressure to include them. She said in *Vibe*, "No, they're not on the album. Only because the album is so narrative. I've revealed myself on this album. So I wasn't going to say, you know, Clef come off the road and let's do this.''

The New York studio that Lauryn had chosen was a dimly lit, wide open, relaxed space. It was a comfortable space, a space that smelled of freedom and freedom was exactly the vibe Lauryn was looking for. Lauryn had warned the musicians that this was not going to be a heavily preplanned quick session. There would be hours and hours of jamming and sheer experimentation in which any and all ideas would be considered. She also assured them that something special would come out of it.

''I wanted to experiment in sound,'' she offered *Entertainment Weekly* on her goals for this album, *The Miseducation of Lauryn Hill*. ''I didn't want it to be too technically perfect.''

The typical session for the album would regularly begin with the musicians just playing. Lauryn, her producer's hat firmly in place, would move smoothly in and out of the control booth, offering suggestions and taking it in stride when something did or did not work. At certain points, she would throw out a rap or a scat vocal fragment, which her players would be quick to pick up on and embellish. When it seemed to make sense, she would cue her engineer to turn on the juice and they would get it on tape.

The musicians on board, many of whom had admitted to having mixed feelings about working with Lauryn, soon warmed to her laid-back way of doing things and appreciated the fact that they were allowed to be real contributors rather than simply hired hands. It was not the way many of those involved in the *Miseducation* sessions were used to working. Engineer Williams remembered the sessions like a big puzzle coming together. A puzzle that was all in Lauryn's head.

Lauryn walked through those early sessions exuding an air of confidence and never showed any outward signs of insecurity to her players. But she stated after the fact that it was not easy being a woman in charge due, in large part, to the fact that she did not have respect initially and that her way of doing things was thinking out music in her head.

Guevara, a keen observer of Hill during what would ultimately be eight full months spread over two studios, sensed that she was a bit tentative. And so it did not surprise him that just about every song on the album was going through at least two or three revisions before Lauryn was satisfied with the results. "It was her first major effort and so she was unsure of herself sometimes," he told Sonic Net. "We would think that stuff was great but she was the perfectionist."

However, through the kind of mental shorthand

that develops in a creative environment, Lauryn could eventually count on getting what she wanted. "The older musicians, especially, often knew what I was talking about and gave me exactly the voicing or the chord I was looking for," she said in *Rolling Stone*.

But the props being shown her in the studio to that point were not enough to put Lauryn completely at ease. She has admitted to a lot of sleepless nights during those early weeks in the studio: She expressed some anxiety that the audience wouldn't be ready or familiar for the honesty in her music. "Fortunately I surrounded myself with a very strong group of people who protected my vision," she told Amazon.com. "Once I got into making the album, I didn't pay attention to any pressure or anyone else's expectancy. I wasn't coming out as a new artist so I felt I had a little more power and control over what I was doing."

And what would ultimately allow Lauryn a comfort zone in the studio was the growing confidence in the power of the words she was writing: "That I could now write about what had happened to me meant that I was over particular situations and that I was healing," she told Amazon.com. "Writing the material on the record was therapeutic. It meant a great deal [to my confidence] that I had clarity which allowed me to be so descriptive. It was totally autobiographical. I knew what I was talking about.''

While *The Miseducation of Lauryn Hill* would turn out to be Lauryn's album in every sense of the word, Lauryn had decided, early on, that the experience would not be a completely memorable one if it was all serious business and had no traces of fun. In an homage to those '60s and '70s classic soul duets, Lauryn placed a call to up-and-coming soul crooner D'Angelo, who zipped into the studio to sing with Lauryn on the steamy ballad ''Nothing Even Matters.'' And when it was determined that the song ''I Used to Love Him'' needed some vocal flavoring, Lauryn rang up reigning diva Mary J. Blige to spice things up.

''When she sings, she feels it,'' remembered Lauryn of their sessions together in *Vibe*. ''For her it's not about perfection. She just strikes that chord.''

A number of songs were written or fine-tuned during the recording of *The Miseducation of Lauryn Hill*, which allowed her the opportunity to explore the true impact of her songs in a different emotional environment. And what Lauryn continued to find was that the simple truths, the strongest emotions, only grew stronger with age.

'' 'Lost Ones' is about a state of mind,'' she reflected on the Amazon.com site. ''I was very young and very naive when I came into the business and probably not as prepared as I should have been. There's a lack of scruples and a lot of money in this business and a tendency on the part of a lot of people to forget you're a person.''

She also told the *Website Reporter*, ''I think most young women can relate to 'Ex-Factor.' You meet a guy and it seems like everything is in place except that one unknown. And in time you find that out. For me it was no matter how I pushed and how perfect I thought we were, it just wasn't there.''

Typical of how Lauryn and her musicians worked their magic together was the development of the song ''Ex-Factor.'' The song had gone through a number of arrangements in its odyssey into the studio. Initially Lauryn had written the song with a more straight-ahead rock sound in mind, and at one point prior to going into the studio the song was given to a rock-and-roll band she had been working with. Consequently, the song ended up having a complete makeover in the studio. Lauryn started with some basic hip-hop and rap grooves but it all seemed too cliche and obvious. So she mentally stepped back and suddenly had an idea—fusing timpani and hip-hop drums for a thick, aggressive backing sound.

Having Zion in the studio with her during many

of the early days helped put Lauryn in a comfort zone. When things got too hectic in the studio, she could always take a step back, feed and change him and momentarily put herself in a different state of mind—one in which she was totally refreshed and energized.

The New York sessions, already a complex process, were the subject of much media and industry speculation. And much of it was not good. Ruffhouse's Chris Schwartz, a longtime Hill supporter who was one of a handful of enthusiastic supporters for Lauryn producing the album, recalled the first time he sat down with the Columbia–Sony Music brass and played a tape of some of the early sessions. He had already put his reputation on the line not only by financing an open-ended recording session and not blinking an eye when Lauryn informed him that it could take a year, but also by not panicking when Lauryn's pregnancy delayed the start of the album. And finally he rejected the idea that a brand-name celebrity producer do the album. Now it was time to put Lauryn's talents and his reputation to the test.

Columbia Records president Donnie Lenner, Sony Music honcho Tommy Mottola and a handful of others bent forward as the tape played out. They listened in silence. They did not look happy.

"They were very basic, raw tracks," remem-

bered Schwartz in the *Philadelphia Inquirer.* "I
knew going in that they were going to be disappointed because they wanted big-name producers
and they were hoping Lauryn was going to do a
Celine Dion/Mariah Carey type thing. I remembered saying 'Hey, bear with us. Chill. This is Lauryn Hill.' "

Lauryn, who by this time had had it with suggestions that Babyface and that kind of slick knob-
turner turn her album into pabulum, appreciated the
fact that Schwartz was sticking his neck out to support her: "Chris said 'I'm going to stay out of your
way,' " she told the *Inquirer.* "That's when I knew
that he respected me and what I was doing. I don't
think I could have done this record someplace
else."

In the meantime there was growing concern in
many quarters that Lauryn's pure, soulful style of
singing would actually benefit from a more R & B
format rather than the highly unpredictable hip-hop
format she was getting in the studio. Controversy
continued over the fact that she was making the
record without Pras and Wyclef. The more negative
press hinted that Lauryn's normally clear vision
had been colored by her recent motherhood. Inevitably most of these comments made their way back
to her and, while she chose to ignore them publicly,
privately she was upset: "Lots of people were talk-

ing to me about going different routes," she told *Rolling Stone*. "I could feel people in my face and I was picking up on bad vibes. I wanted a place where there were good vibes."

Lauryn's thoughts turned to Jamaica and the Tuff Gong Studios. It was the legendary home of Ro's father and the home of his brothers Steven, Ziggy and Justin and their children. Lauryn sensed that having family around her would help her relax and, by association, create.

The studios were also an attraction. The ghosts of many reggae legends were alive within those walls. Magic had been made at Tuff Gong and she would, most certainly, turn to its legacy and find inspiration. But the major selling point was that she would be making her music thousands of miles away from the prying eyes of record company executives who still, she reasoned, looked at her more as a product than an individual talent.

But for all her optimism about relocating, Lauryn was feeling scattered as the plane carrying her and her musicians touched down in Jamaica. While the sessions in New York had "been there" artistically, something in the emotion of the music had been missing. For Lauryn there had to be a purpose in the music—something personal to justify what she was doing. Otherwise she would just be giving the record company what it wanted and she would be shortchanging herself. Yes, her songs had their messages. But somehow she felt detached from them and that was not going to be good enough.

The magic that Lauryn hoped would make this album special appeared to her on her very first day in the Tuff Gong Studios. Lauryn had been playing around with some lyrics to a song that would ultimately become ''Lost Ones''—a resigned, disillusioned ode to getting ahead and leaving others behind. Lauryn had come up with a single line: ''It's funny how money change a situation.'' She repeated the line several times; changing the rhythm and tone in an attempt to get the emotion behind the words. Other lines would slowly tumble out of her consciousness and into words. When she had enough lines down, Lauryn added a basic drum machine backing and began to rap over the drum. She frowned. It was getting there but it was not quite where she wanted it to be.

Lauryn took a break and sprawled out on a couch in a living room adjacent to the studio. She was immediately surrounded by fifteen young children, the collected children of Bob Marley's sons. Lauryn smiled and began talking to them. Finally, in a moment of divine inspiration, she began softly to rap out the lines to ''Lost Ones.'' The children sat for a moment, transfixed by the words. Then they began cautiously to repeat the last word of each line. They became bolder each time Lauryn repeated the rap and were soon chiming in almost as if they knew the song by heart.

The singer was surprised and, perhaps, just a bit amazed at how these tiny boys and girls, who did not have a care in the world, were suddenly so into a song that told of emotionally trying times. For Lauryn, the missing piece of the puzzle suddenly fell into place. Now she knew what *The Miseducation of Lauryn Hill* was all about.

The recording of the album suddenly took on the vision of a voyage of self-discovery in which innocence, disillusionment and finally inner peace played out against the forces of heartless and soulless individuals and finally the powerful intervention of God in her life. Lauryn immediately began a renewed burst of writing. She also began to read the Bible regularly for the comfort the words afforded her. The album had suddenly turned from a mere exercise in creativity to a self-examination of her heart and soul that, she would relate, provided comfort and revelation.

"It [the album] ended up saying a lot about what people didn't know about me," she related to *Rolling Stone* of her newfound insights during the recording of *The Miseducation of Lauryn Hill*. "The songs are more for me than they are for anybody else."

With the lyrical and emotional focus in place, Lauryn redirected her efforts in the direction of a live musical feel. Such exotic instruments as celestas, harps and timpani drums weaved exotic and very personal musical passages through the expected R & B guitar-bass-drums lineup. There were many takes because Lauryn insisted that overdubs would mute the emotion and that only the perfect live take would do.

"I always had an appetite for live musicianship," she said of the process in an *Ebony* interview. "The human element had to be there. I want a real piano even if it's a little out of tune. Sometimes that's the beauty of the whole thing."

The beauty and substance of Lauryn Hill's songs slowly began to manifest themselves. "Every Ghetto, Every City" encapsulated the feeling and the love of the streets that she grew up in. "Ex-Factor" and "When It Hurts So Bad" often had Lauryn tearful as she faced, head-on, the loves that had scarred her. And finally there was "To Zion," Lauryn's oh-so-personal ode to her son and, by association, her hope for his future and hers. "To Zion" meant a lot to Lauryn and so, when she left Jamaica and returned to the States for a last bit of fine-tuning of the album tracks, that song was still in a state of flux.

Guevara recalled that his mixer status was suddenly elevated to coproducer/cowriter on "To Zion." Easily the most personal song on the album, the lyrics to "To Zion" had come to Lauryn while she had been sick with the flu and had become terrified at the prospect of passing the illness on to her infant son. Her mother had responded to Lauryn's fears by simply telling her to relax. "And that's when the lyrics just came to me," remembers Lauryn in *Vibe*.

"Lauryn had already written the words to 'To Zion' but she hadn't gotten around to doing any of the music yet," recalled Guevara in Sonic Net. "I had already started to play around with some music for the track and when she heard what I had come up with she said 'This is it.' "

The musical backing included a part for some delicate flamenco guitar passages. "I had this guy who I actually wanted to lay down some flamenco guitar on it. But, at one point, Lauryn said she had a connection to Carlos Santana. I was excited when she mentioned it. That's the kind of opportunity that you don't want to miss."

It was hard to tell whether Lauryn or Ché had the biggest lump in their throat the day Carlos Santana flew into New York for the express purpose of laying down a haunting flamenco-style backing to "To Zion." Santana, a spiritual person in his own right, had to hold back tears as he heard the song for the first time.

"When I heard the song, it broke me up," the superstar guitarist stated in *Entertainment Weekly*. "The world is telling her to go this way and your record company says you should be doing this but your heart says 'go this way,' so you go that way. It takes a lot of courage to do that."

Guevara still gets misty-eyed when he thinks about the song and how it turned out to be an emotional high point for Lauryn: " 'To Zion' is truly a reflection of her and her mind state she was in when she made the album. She had a lot of emotions and stuff she wanted to express and that all came out in what she was writing."

Lauryn's spiritual reawakening during the recording of *The Miseducation of Lauryn Hill* resulted in her finally acknowledging publicly that Rohan Marley was, in fact, the father of her child. It was a freeing experience for both of them. In one fell swoop, it answered all the questions and put the rumors to rest. But what did not change was their insistence on keeping their relationship low-key. She did not want their relationship "to be just another media event."

"We're still very private," she explained candidly in the pages of *Vibe*. "I still don't like to talk about it. I want to love him away from the lights, camera, action and I want him to love me away from all that."

Lauryn went into the year 1998 in a state of bliss. She was with the man she loved and together they had produced the most perfect child. The icing on the cake was an album that she felt not only represented her life but also changed the perception of rap and hip-hop music. But the question remained for Lauryn: Would putting her heart and soul on the chopping block of public opinion result in total acceptance or heartbreaking rejection?

Lauryn Hill was not sure. She admitted to a *Spin* reporter, "I was thinking that hip-hop and R & B as we know know them aren't as personal as the music I had wanted to make. I'm nervous that people are not going to be able to relate [to the music] or [are going to] think that I'm a Martian."

Lauryn crossed her fingers . . . and prayed.

SEVEN

Props

Lauryn Hill spent the first two months of 1998 walking an emotional tightrope. Waiting for *The Miseducation of Lauryn Hill* to drop was hell. She knew in her heart that she had done the right thing by putting her emotions to music. Even if the record tanked she would be happy for the experience. But, God! She really wanted everybody to love it!

Critics were already lining up to make their predictions. Some, without having heard a song, were already predicting the album would be at the top of the ten-best list at year's end. A small, cynical contingent was, likewise, predicting that Lauryn, without Clef and Pras at her back, would not only falter as a solo artist but alienate the Fugee fans who had supported her in the process.

And with so little concrete material to write about, it was inevitable that the press, jumping on a smattering of lyrics and second- and third-hand reports from people who had heard the record, created a controversy, or rather a feud, between Lauryn and Wyclef. The evidence, they surmised, was in the lyrics of the songs. Is Wyclef's song "To All the Girls" from his *The Carnival* album about his alleged romance and eventual blowup with Lauryn? Is "Ex-Factor" and "Lost Ones" Lauryn's way of telling Wyclef and Pras that it's all over, personally and professionally?

Initially Lauryn denied that the songs were veiled attacks on her mates. Eventually she began to hint at "issues" and "different dynamics." Then there were the ominous denials that the songs were not about being "upset" or being "stabbed in the back." However, Lauryn, perhaps tiring of all the game-playing, finally came clean and admitted the fact that there was trouble in paradise and that the future of the Fugees was very much in doubt.

She admitted that she had not spoken with Clef or Pras "for a long time" and that they were "not very close right now." But she did hold out hope for the future in a recent *Rolling Stone* interview: "I think in our own sweet time we're gonna get in a room and talk to each other about all our issues and make some music. But that can't happen prematurely or I think it would damage things.''

As if things could not get any more hectic, in February 1998 Lauryn discovered that she was once again pregnant. Lauryn and Rohan were once again surprised and happy. They had talked about having ''lots of children'' and Lauryn had joked in the wake of Zion's birth that ''Rohan likes that I've got hips and a little bit more on top now.'' Lauryn happily calculated that she would have her second child a couple of months after she released *The Miseducation of Lauryn Hill*. But she knew which event was ultimately the most important: She said a child puts everything in perspective and if she stopped enjoying the music business she could quit and not look back.

At the moment, however, Lauryn was enjoying a self-imposed period of relative leisure. There had been the expected offers to tour—her first solo tour, in advance of the release of the album. But Lauryn did not want to risk her unborn child to the rigors of the road.

She was nowhere near a studio; although she was constantly on the phone dealing with big and small issues relating to the upcoming release of her album. Lauryn was also using the time to get reacquainted with the idea of acting again. Scripts had not really been piling up on her doorstep but every once in a while something would arrive that would peak her interest. One such script called *Beloved*, based on a Toni Morrison novel, struck a nerve. Lauryn loved its sense of history, drama and its well-drawn characters. She liked the idea that a couple of her favorite people, Oprah Winfrey and Danny Glover, were signed to the project. Unfortunately the timing of her pregnancy and the strenuous nature of the shoot prevented her from doing the picture.

But Lauryn did lay the groundwork for future adventures on the big screen when she formed her own film production company, Black Market Films, in which she would develop projects that she would produce and, possibly, star in. Rumors immediately began flying that the first Lauryn Hill movies were going to be black science fiction movies. Lauryn said sci-fi was a definite possibility at some point and she was considering doing a small part in an independent film called *Restaurant*. But, for the time being, she was looking for the best script, period.

"I want to treat films the same way I treat music," she explored in *Ebony*. "I don't want to do it just for the sake of doing it. I'd like to do something new and original."

But for now Lauryn was content to hole up in her South Orange, New Jersey, home. She played

with Zion and marveled at his growth, watched as
her belly swelled with child for a second time and
added credence to the at-large vision of Lauryn Hill
as one of the plain folks. She would hang with her
childhood friends and smile contentedly as her parents and Ro catered to her every need.

On her twenty-third birthday she reflected on her
arrival as "an experienced, well-traveled woman."
To her way of thinking, Lauryn had passed through
every conceivable emotion and experienced every
possible up and down in her life and career. That
she had emerged, at such a young age, at the end
of the tunnel and in a state of grace was, to her
way of thinking, God's will.

"I'm very happy," she announced in *Vibe*. "I'm
with a good man, and a child, and a family. And I
don't have the fear of losing my job. The only person who can fire me is God."

Lauryn's sense of inner peace and tranquillity
carried her effortlessly through the ensuing months.
The physical discomfort and the emotional mood
swings were there but not with the ferocity of her
previous birth. The upcoming release of her album
and the attendant rush of media interest kept Lauryn's mind focused. However, as the calendar
pages turned to August and the album was finally
a mere three weeks away from hitting the curb,
Lauryn began to feel nervous. She knew she had

made a wonderful album. She only hoped the kids on the street felt the same way.

The Miseducation of Lauryn Hill dropped on August 25, 1998. The response to it was immediate and joyous. The *Los Angeles Times*, albeit in a not-quite-rave review, acknowledged Lauryn's rap as "fierce and authoritative." Street-savvy *The Source* proclaimed Lauryn "the flyest MC ever." The straitlaced *New York Times* called her album "visionary."

The raves continued. *Entertainment Weekly* announced that "Hill has made an album of often astonishing power and strength." *USA Today* called *Miseducation* "a whole album that is a listening pleasure." *Rolling Stone* called the album "a hip-hop soul classic."

Miseducation exploded onto the top of the coveted *Billboard* charts; setting a record for first-week sales by a female artist and was certified gold, platinum and then triple platinum in a matter of weeks. Radio was all over the album, playing "To Zion" almost as a courtesy but also getting deep into the album's tougher cuts. "Superstar" broke out of the pack and onto the playlists early. The bounce first single, "Doo Wop" followed the album to the top of the charts. By September you could not turn on a radio, regardless of format, and not hear Lauryn's music coming out of the speakers.

In a seemingly endless round of press interviews, Lauryn tried any number of ways to describe her feelings about making *Miseducation* and coming to grips with its massive success. Depending on the moment the question was asked and what degree of exhaustion she was in as she entered her eighth month of pregnancy, Lauryn could be religious, real world or somewhere in between with her response.

"It wasn't someone telling me what I felt and it wasn't someone writing for me," she explained at one point to *Spin*. "It was exactly what I felt the moment I felt it."

And she made no bones about the fact that the turning point for her, spiritually and creatively, began when Rohan came into her life. She could rattle off the obvious inner qualities of the man at the drop of a hat: his kind heart, his sense of humor, his sincerity. But the man in her life also gathered major props for his timing: Ro had come into her life when she was not looking for anyone but needed someone very badly.

But while they were a good match, Lauryn and Rohan, mere weeks before Lauryn made ready to give birth to her second child, had not yet decided to make their union legal. She had offered that Rohan is there for her and her children in every way and that they have discussed marriage and will tie the knot at some as yet undetermined point: "We haven't been in front of a minister yet but we will be soon," she revealed in *Ebony*. "Our marriage right now is more of a spiritual one. One thing is certain, when we do get married it will be in private. Our relationship isn't a publicity stunt. We don't do things just to get into the paper. We just do things to live."

And one of the things Lauryn was doing to live as she was counting down the days to motherhood was once again producing a single track for a recent acquaintance of hers, Whitney Houston. Houston, promoting the release of the album *My Love Is Your Love* had to laugh when she recalled on MTV News the day Lauryn waddled in to produce the title cut: "She walked into the studio and she was like this round. So she walks in there and I say 'Lauryn, you okay?' she said 'Oh yeah, I'm ready to do this.' She stayed in the studio twenty hours after I had left. I kept calling her, saying 'Lauryn, you have to go home.' And she kept saying 'No, I have to do this.' "

Lauryn Hill went into labor on November 12, 1998. Within a matter of hours, a daughter, Selah Louise, was born. Under different circumstances Lauryn would have taken six months off to bond with her daughter. But *Miseducation* was continuing to invoke a major emotion on the psyche of music lovers and so her time away from the public eye was limited. Lauryn returned to the publicity trail with all the fervor of a fiery preacher addressing her congregation. Lauryn Hill was not merely selling a product. She was putting her soul on display.

Lauryn, during this period, took a tentative first step to getting back with her brothers Wyclef and Pras when she agreed to appear with them in the movie *Ghetto Supastar*. The project, set up through Madonna's production company and titled after Pras's solo album, tells the story of a Brooklyn rapper trying to make it in the business. The group will, most likely, play rap–hip-hop musicians, although without a script it is too early to report any particulars. What is known is that Lauryn was thrilled at the opportunity to act.

Lauryn also announced that she would be going into the studio to sing on a pair of songs for the upcoming Mary J. Blige album as a way of saying thanks for the singer's contribution to *Miseducation*.

For Lauryn, 1998 could not be ending on a higher of highs. Yet on November 23, 1998, Lauryn Hill was sued for two million dollars.

The suit, filed by the musicians Vada Nobles, Johari Newton, Tejumold Newton and Rasheem Pugh, claimed that Lauryn had improperly taken sole production and songwriting credits for the fourteen songs on her album. The lawsuit further charged that a hundred-thousand-dollar music publishing deal that the four musicians signed in November 1997 was designed to cheat them out of credit on Hill's album. The musicians offered that they had tapes and documents that they would produce at a trial to prove their case.

A number of people sprang to Lauryn's defense, citing the musicians' suit as a calculated attempt to take advantage of her success. One of her most adamant defenders against the charges was her *Miseducation* engineer Gordon Williams who, almost immediately, went on the record by telling *Spin*, "Definitely the driving force behind the record was Hill."

According to those in her inner circle, Hill was devastated by the charges and, not surprisingly, angry at the way she was repaid for the opportunity she had given them. However, there were no public statements from her regarding the lawsuit that, as the year drew to a close, was winding its way slowly through the legal system.

With the universal popularity of *The Miseducation of Lauryn Hill*, the inevitable call for tours and live appearances on television began to flood in. Lauryn, however, was still bonding with her daughter and so was, while already mentally preparing to do her first solo tour sometime after the first of the year, a bit hesitant about doing anything that would take her far from home or into an uncomfortable interview situation. The last thing she wanted to do was end up fueling the Fugees feud fire, which, thankfully, had finally begun to die down.

One of the appearances Lauryn did agree to do was the *Rosie O'Donnell Show*, a lightweight talk show in which she could do a song or two and avoid any probing questions. Something else that looked like fun was a slot on *Saturday Night Live*.

Lauryn was sitting in the *Saturday Night Live* dressing room, her eyes nervously scanning the room and her entourage. They were assuring her that everything was going to be alright. Suddenly the door opened and one of the producers walked in and handed her a script. She smiled bravely as the producer made small talk about how she'd love it and then walked out. Lauryn looked at the script.

She was not happy.

Lauryn had arrived for the rehearsals for her musical number and had stayed to watch the *SNL* regulars go through their preparations for the show's skits. She found herself laughing at the funnier bits and, at one point, was approached by some of the members of the show and asked if she wanted to be in a sketch they were working on. Lauryn giggled and then thought that it might be fun to do a little bit of acting. So she agreed to look at whatever they came up with.

Lauryn was now looking at a script entitled "Pimp Chat." The idea of a street hustler with a talk show was mildly amusing. But the part they had written for her was not. They wanted her to play a crazed ho. She was not comfortable with the idea. Would she do it anyway?

Lauryn thanked the show's producers but said she did not feel comfortable doing the skit. Whether they understood or not was not important. Quite simply, she felt too connected to her music to do anything that might compromise its message.

Christmas 1998 was a joyous and religious time for Lauryn. A Christmas tree with a black Mary and Joseph at its base and a black angel on top anchored a far corner of her living room. Gathered for a night of good cheer, good fellowship and, into the next morning, a little bit of work, were her parents, her children, her lover and a wide assortment of musicians, managers and "just plain folks." At the precise moment, the guests joined hands around a table overflowing with food and Lauryn entered the room. She quietly blessed the food and thanked God for her good fortune.

The next morning Lauryn, headphones on and

grooving to a funky rhythm track in the bowels of a Manhattan recording studio, was working on a rhyme that was inserted into a new Curtis Mayfield song for the *Mod Squad* movie soundtrack. A pair of lyric-strewn legal pads at her feet attested to the fact that she was not going to let anything but a perfect rhyme end up on a song by one of her heroes. Finally she had the rap where she wanted it and the engineer played back the song so that Lauryn could figure when it would be time to jump in.

The *Mod Squad* gig was a perfect example of the doors that stardom can open for someone. Her phone was ringing off the hook with offers for soundtrack and production work. Lauryn was being picky but she obviously relished being a part of all facets of the music business. "I don't always like to be the person in front," she once remarked. "I like all facets of creating."

Lauryn spent a peaceful New Year's Eve in South Orange, surrounded by her family and friends. She was in good spirits. Motherhood seemed to agree with her. The new year would be an exciting one. Lauryn had decided that she would tour solo for the first time beginning in February and, although it was against her nature to brag, she was quietly confident that she would be acknowledged by the Grammys. Those would be the loud times. Those would be the bomb. Right now being mother, child and lover was all her soul needed. She said, "I'm definitely in a beautiful and stable place," she told *Essence*. "I have everything I need."

And with that spiritual state of mind came a continued attention to her charitable organization, the Refugee Project. From the outset, Lauryn had taken her approach to doing good works seriously. She was not going to be one of those celebrities who started something in name only and then would be around only to sign a check. Lauryn, schedule permitting, made herself available for every photo opportunity and interview that would ultimately do the Refugee Project and the needy people it served some good. And she was constantly calling in favors from record-company executives and fellow artists to help keep her projects afloat. Lauryn Hill's real-world attitude and unselfish nature was never more evident in those moments when she stopped her busy world to help the less fortunate.

Lauryn, during this period, was also encouraged by the fact that Wyclef and Pras had been making encouraging noises in the press about getting together and doing another Fugees's album in 1999. Although, realistically, under the most ideal of circumstances, Lauryn did not see the group getting into the studio again until the year 2000.

It was a cold Saturday night in New York. But inside a nondescript rehearsal hall, it was hot! hot! hot! Lauryn was swaying back and forth to a raw, rhythm-heavy backing that was being laid down by her band. Satisfied that an appropriate groove had been laid down, she moved to the middle of the group and started singing. In the next few hours, Lauryn and her band would run through every song she would be singing on her upcoming tour. The songs were sounding tight. Lauryn shuddered as she imagined what it would be like singing ''To Zion,'' ''Lost Ones'' and ''Ex-Factor'' in front of an audience of thousands. It was the chill of anticipation and triumph.

Her mental high was suddenly interrupted by the wailing of sirens racing through the streets. Expecting them to race past and disappear, Lauryn turned and was about to have another go at her music, when the sirens welled up loud right in front of the studio and then stopped. Immediately her street curiosity was aroused and she wandered over to the studio's main entrance and poked her head outside.

There was a fire truck nearby and a couple of police squad cars. A team of firemen had layed out the hose and was spraying a steady stream of

EIGHT

Around the World

"She was hysterical," recalled New York City police officer Jose Segura to the *National Enquirer* regarding the moment Lauryn emerged from the studio and saw the car ablaze. "She thought he was still in the car."

The officers on the scene went quickly to her side and informed her that Rohan had been rescued from the car and that he was inside the ambulance, which was headed for a nearby hospital. The officers further calmed her by saying that it looked like Rohan was suffering only from smoke inhalation and that he would be okay. That did little to reassure Lauryn, whose face was streaked with tears. She immediately got into a car and followed the ambulance to the hospital where the whole story of Lauryn and Ro's near-tragedy began to unfold.

At one point in the evening, Lauryn had indicated that she was getting ready to call it a night and Rohan had gone outside to warm up their car. But, as these things often happen, the rehearsal kept going longer than expected and a very tired Rohan nodded off to sleep. While he slept, the car engine sparked and eventually erupted into flames. Rohan coughed and sputtered and awoke to find the inside of the car completely filled with smoke. He attempted to get out of the car but, to his horror, discovered that an electrical malfunction, caused by the fire, made it impossible to unlock the doors or open the windows.

In a complete panic he began banging on the windows, trying to draw the attention of passers-by. Fortunately, Officer Segura and his partner happened to be passing through the area on patrol and spotted Rohan's hands up against the window. Officer Segura smashed open the window with his nightstick and the two officers forced open the driver's side door and pulled Rohan to safety.

Lauryn had calmed down somewhat by the time she reached the hospital, but was a picture of fear and concern as she sat waiting for the doctor to come into the waiting room and give her the thumbs-up. Then she cried tears of happiness as she raced into the recovery room to be with her man.

Rohan's near-death experience served only to strengthen Lauryn's religion. Hours later, she reportedly told a family friend, "For a second there, I thought he was dead. But I believe it's a sign from God [that he's alive]. God spared my love for a reason and I believe it's so we can get married. I'm certain of that now."

However, while certain, the couple did not seem in too much of a hurry to walk down the aisle. Lauryn had often proclaimed that Rohan was already "like a husband" and that their relationship was already like a married couple's with only the license missing. In fact Lauryn was candid in saying, in the aftermath of her lover's near-death experience, that "Rohan has always wanted to get married but I was the one that wanted to wait. But after what almost happened to him, I'm not waiting any longer."

Lauryn and Rohan would, in fact, wait as the reality of her career once again stepped to the fore. In mid-January 1999, Lauryn flew to Japan with the Fugees where a flurry of concerts and press interviews in Asia and Europe would test the waters of Lauryn Hill as a worldwide presence. Fugees's albums had always done well in Europe and

Asia and that momentum had carried over into her solo debut as *The Miseducation of Lauryn Hill* had debuted platinum in both Canada and Japan and had hit the charts at number two in England and Norway and number three in France.

But this would be the first time Lauryn would be testing the waters alone on a concert stage. Advance-ticket sales had assured that the three shows in Japan would be sellouts. But that did not stop Lauryn from pacing like a cat backstage at The Budokhan on January 21 as she prepared to go on-stage alone for the very first time. As Lauryn stepped out on the stage to thunderous applause, her nerves completely left her. For the next two hours, Lauryn took the audience on a melodic trip through her solo album, the odd bit of Fugees's business and a selection of old favorites. According to reviews of that show and the subsequent concerts at the Forum and an arena in Osaka, Lauryn was electric—alternately mellow and angry, belting out the message songs and the more personal tunes with a range of legitimate emotions. Lauryn was particularly thrilled that her songs of inner peace, happiness and defiance had traveled so well over-seas.

"I look at it as serendipity," she told *Rolling Stone*. "It's a wonderful, incredible thing and it confirms a few things for me. It confirms that my experiences are a lot more universal than I thought and that people are ready to hear the truth.''

The successes continued as Lauryn wowed audiences in London and chalked up rave reviews and gained points with the European and Asian press for her candor, personality and patience as she willingly answered the same questions she had been answering in America. With the success of Europe and Asia ringing in her ears, Lauryn returned to the United States in early February.

She took a couple of days off in South Orange to be a full-time mother to her children and then began to iron out the logistics of the U.S. portion of her tour, which would begin February 18 in Detroit and then swing out across the country for a series of shows that would carry Lauryn into April. Lauryn was also mentally preparing to take time off the road on February 24 when she would be performing the song ''To Zion'' at the Grammy Awards and, hopefully, walking off with an armful of awards.

Lauryn got a preview of what her Grammy night might be like on February 13 in Pasadena, California, when the prestigious NAACP Image Awards selected her as Outstanding Female Artist, Outstanding New Artist and named *The Miseducation of Lauryn Hill* the year's Best Album. But the award that meant more to Lauryn than any of the others she received that night came near the end of the evening when she was awarded the President's Award for her charity work with the Refugee Camp.

The applause had barely died down at the NAACP Awards when Lauryn was on a plane bound for Miami where she performed, along with Ziggy Marley and Erykah Badu at the sixth annual Bob Marley Caribbean Festival. For Lauryn this show brought back memories of the Fugees's performance in Haiti. It was a feeling she liked. But it was also a feeling Lauryn was almost too tired to feel.

Lauryn had come off the road in a state of euphoria and near-exhaustion. Too many planes, too many shows and not enough time for herself and her family. She would occasionally look frail and all the makeup in the world could not hide the lines under her eyes from lack of sleep. More than one member of her crew began to worry privately that maybe trying to do it all at once was beginning to catch up with her.

Engineer Gordon Williams was one of those, during the height of Lauryn Hill mania, to go public with his concerns when he told *Spin*: "She's a workaholic. She just doesn't stop. To be a mother two times, and then have all this stuff going on is crazy. Sometimes I just look at her and go 'Lauryn, take it easy.' ''

However, Lauryn steadfastly denied that she was about to break under the stress of stardom and motherhood. She proclaimed that she was in control of what was going on in her life and that she was not going to do anything that would ultimately be detrimental to herself or her children. Those in Lauryn's inner circle tended to believe her.

Lauryn Hill's first ever solo U.S. date, at the Fox Theatre in Detroit, Michigan, was a sellout, and a raucous one at that. The sounds of feet-stomping, hand-clapping and all manner of hoots, whistles and screams were rapidly reaching jet engine volume—and it was easily heard backstage where Lauryn, in an upbeat mood that was both excitement and nervous energy, waited for her cue to go onstage. The house lights finally dimmed and Lauryn sauntered onstage.

The air was electric as the singer launched into— her first song, and it stayed that way throughout the show. Lauryn was in total command, seemingly able to raise or lower the emotion of the crowd with a look or a move or a fiery rap. She had been concerned that the mellower and more introspective moments in her music might suffer in a live, not-very-intimate setting. However, Lauryn quickly

discovered that the audience was into the music
rather than just the experience and so they could
be counted on to be attentive and respectful when
a song like "To Zion" was sung. Lauryn Hill had
opened up her heart and soul on a dark night in
Detroit. By the end of the show, everyone had seen
the light.

The same scenario played itself out two days
later in Chicago and two days after that in St.
Louis. Reviewers were falling all over themselves
to sing her praises. Now, if only the Grammy
judges would do the same! Lauryn had gone
through the "being nominated is the most important thing" phase and was now quietly optimistic
that she would end up carrying home a few of the
prized statuettes.

It was cloudy, cold and slightly overcast on February 24 in Los Angeles. Lauryn was excited as
she hopped into the limo that would carry her to
the ceremonies. As her ride snaked through Los
Angeles, Lauryn, in the backseat, was, according
to reports filtering out of her entourage, exhibiting
a wide array of emotions. There was the excitement
and the expected butterflies. And, at moments,
there was a sense of peace and serenity that seemed
to envelop the young woman. It was as if all the
trials and tribulations in her personal and professional life had suddenly led her to this point—a

happy, rewarding life with much more still to come.

"Right now I have time to build," she reflected in *Vibe*. "And I am not afraid."

Lauryn Hill had played by her rules. And won.

And the Winner Is . . .

Lauryn, with Rohan on her arm, was wide-eyed as she walked down the red carpet of the Shrine Auditorium in Los Angeles. The crowd of fans began cheering the moment they spotted her. Lauryn, dressed in a long dress, a simple sleeveless top and a red knit cap, smiled and waved back. The papparazzi were out in force, flashing strobe light–strength flashbulbs in her face as they struggled for the best possible camera angle.

Inside, they found their seats in the star-studded front rows. Off to one side Will Smith and his wife, Jada Pinkett Smith, were just settling into their seats. A couple of rows farther up, Celine Dion was exchanging pleasantries with composer James Horner, one half of the creative team responsible for her monster hit "My Heart Will Go On." And sitting nearby was Wyclef.

Finally the lights went down and an orchestrated musical backing swelled up. Lauryn settled back into her seat. She was ready for whatever was to come.

She would not be waiting long. The R & B categories were announced early in the program. Lauryn had been the odds-on favorite to run the table in this group. And, in short order, Lauryn was walking up to the stage to accept Grammys for Best R & B Album for *The Miseducation of Lauryn Hill,* R & B Song for "Doo Wop (That Thing)" and Best R & B Vocal Performance.

Later in the evening, her smile got even bigger when, after winning the Grammy for Best Rock Album, Sheryl Crow, in her acceptance speech, said, "I want Lauryn Hill to produce my next album."

The anticipation and excitement grew as the awards ceremony continued. Admittedly there had not been much of a surprise so far. Lauryn had captured the honors the press had speculated she had a lock on. But the gold rings, Album of the Year and Best New Artist, were not a sure thing. The competition was stiff and anything could happen.

"And the winner is . . . Lauryn Hill!"

Lauryn's eyes went wide in surprise. She had not expected the rush of emotion she was experiencing as she stood to thunderous applause, received a congratulatory kiss from Rohan and walked up to the stage. The audience held their breath. The last time Lauryn had been to a Grammy ceremony, she had been militant and defiant in her acceptance speech. She had not been that way in accepting her earlier honors that evening, but what better opportunity to make a political or social statement than while accepting one of the music industry's top honors.

Lauryn strode to the microphone and said, "I'm going to do something a little bit different." She opened the Bible she held in her hand and read a passage from Psalm 40. Then she thanked God, Rohan and all the expected management and record company people and, in a conciliatory gesture, the Fugees. "And finally I want to thank the kids for not spilling stuff on my outfit." She laughed before walking offstage to more applause and into a quick costume change to all white for her live performance of "To Zion."

This was a special moment for Lauryn. She sang the song with strength and emotion. To her right Carlos Santana, who had picked out the haunting flamenco passages on the record, was smiling as he duplicated the licks live.

Lauryn finished the song and then stood, breath-lessly, backstage as the ceremonies concluded with the final award of the evening, Album of the Year. "And the winner is . . . Lauryn Hill! *The Miseducation of Lauryn Hill*." Lauryn now held the record for the most Grammys in a single year by a female.

Lauryn walked back out. "This is so amazing," she said excitedly. "This is crazy because it's hip-hop!" She once again thanked everybody involved in making her record. Finally Lauryn Hill was humbled.

"Stay positive," she proclaimed. "Only God is great."

Discography

LAURYN HILL

U.S. RELEASES

The Miseducation of Lauryn Hill *(1998)*
SONGS: Intro, Lost Ones, Ex-Factor, To Zion, Doo Wop (That Thing), Superstar, Final Hour, When It Hurts So Bad, I Used to Love Him, Forgive Them Father, Every Ghetto, Every City, Nothing Even Matters, Everything Is Everything, The Miseducation of Lauryn Hill, Can't Take My Eyes off You
PRODUCER: Lauryn Hill

Doo Wop *(1998)*
SONGS: Doo Wop (That Thing) (Rad Mix), Lost Ones, Doo Wop (That Thing) (Gor Mix), Tell Him (Live), Can't Take My Eyes off You
PRODUCER: Lauryn Hill

Love Jones (Soundtrack) *(1997)*
SONG: The Sweetest Thing
PRODUCER: Lauryn Hill

IMPORT RELEASES

The Miseducation of Lauryn Hill (Plus Bonus Tracks) *(1998)* Japanese Import
SONGS: Roll Call Intro, Lost Ones, Love Int, X-Factor, Two Zaion, How Many of U Have Everin, Doo Lip, Intelligent Woman Skit, Sperstar, Final Hr, When It Hurts So Bad, Luv Is Confusion Skit, I Used to Luv Him, Forgive Me Father, What Do U Think Iut, Every Ghetto, Every City, Nothing Even Matters, Everything Is Everything, Miseducation, Tell Him (Live)
PRODUCER: Lauryn Hill

Doo Wop *(1998)* German Import
SONGS: Doo Wop (That Thing) (Rad Mix), Lost Ones, Doo Wop (That Thing) (Gor Mix), Doo Wop (That Thing) (Ins Mix)
PRODUCER: Lauryn Hill

Doo Wop (That Thing) Part One *(1998)*
England Import
SONGS: Doo Wop (That Thing) (Rad Mix), Lost Ones, Forgive Them Father A Cappella
PRODUCER: Lauryn Hill

Doo Wop (That Thing) Part Two *(1998)*
England Import

SONGS: Doo Wop (That Thing), Doo Wop (Gordon's Dub), Doo Wop
PRODUCER: Lauryn Hill

THE FUGEES

U.S. RELEASES

The Score (Explicit Version) *(1996)*
SONGS: Red Intro, How Many Mics, Ready or Not, Zealots, The Beast, Fu-Gee-La, Family Business, Killing Me Softly, The Score, The Mask, Cowboys, No Woman, No Cry, Manifesto/Outro, Fu-Gee-La (Refugee Camp Remix), Fu-Gee-La (Sly & Robbie Mix), Mista Mista
PRODUCERS: Wyclef Jean, Lauryn Hill, Shawn King, Saleem Remi, John Forte, Diamond D., Handel Tucker

The Score (Edited Version) *(1996)*
SONGS: Red Intro, How Many Mics, Ready or Not, Zealots, The Beast, Fu-Gee-La, Family Business, Killing Me Softly, The Score, The Mask, Cowboys, No Woman, No Cry, Manifesto/Outro, Fu-Gee-La (Refugee Camp Remix), Fu-Gee-La (Sly & Robbie Mix), Mista Mista
PRODUCERS: Wyclef Jean, Lauryn Hill, Shawn

King, Saleem Remi, John Forte, Diamond D., Handel Tucker

Bootleg Versions *(1996)*

SONGS: Ready or Not, Nappy Heads, Don't Cry, Dry Your Eyes, Vocab, Killing Me Softly, No Woman, No Cry, Vocab

PRODUCERS: Clark Kent, Wyclef Jean, Prakazrel Michel, Saleem Remi

Blunted on Reality *(1994)*

SONGS: Introduction, Nappy Heads, Blunted Interlude, Recharge, Freestyle Interlude, Vocab, Special News Bulletin Interlude, Boof Baf, Temple, How Hard Is It?, Harlem Chit Chat Interlude, Some Seek Stardom, Giggles, Da Kid from Haiti Interlude, Refugees on the Mic, Living like There Ain't No Tomorrow, Shout Outs from the Block, Nappy Heads (Remix)

PRODUCERS: Rashad Muhammad, Le Jam Productions, Inc., Brand X, Wyclef Jean, Prakazrel Michel, Khalis Bayyan, Stephen Walker, Jerry

Fu-Gee-La *(1996)*

SONGS: Fu-Gee-La (album version), Fu-Gee-La (album version instrumental), Fu-Gee-La (Refugee Camp Remix), Fu-Gee-La (Refugee Camp Remix Instrumental), Fu-Gee-La (album version, a cap-

pella, cassette only), Fu-Gee-La (north side mix), Fu-Gee-La (Sly & Robbie mix), How Many Mics, How Many Mics (a cappella, cassette only)
PRODUCERS: same as *The Score* credits

Vocab *(1994)*
SONGS: Vocab (Remix), Vocab (Refugees Hip-Hop Remix), Vocab (Refugees Acoustic Remix), Refugees on the Mic (Remix), Vocab (Remix Instrumental), Vocab (Salaam's Acoustic Remix), Vocab (Vibey Remix), Nappy Heads (Mad Spider Mix)
PRODUCERS: same as *Blunted on Reality* credits

Funkmaster Flex: The Master Tapes Vol. 1 *(1995)*
SONGS: Freestyle
PRODUCER: Funkmaster Flex

When We Were Kings—Soundtrack *(1997)*
SONGS: Rumble in the Jungle (The Fugees, featuring A Tribe Called Quest, Busta Rhymes and Forte)
PRODUCERS: David Sonenberg, Scot McCracken

Pump Ya Fist: Hip-Hop Inspired by the Movie *Panther (1995)*
SONGS: Recognition

PRODUCERS: KRS-One, Big Jess, Stud Doogie, Ikuan The Dreaded Wonder, Easy Mo Bee

Tibetan Freedom Concert *(1997)*
SONGS: Fu-Gee-La
PRODUCER: Pat McCarthy

Filmography

MOTION PICTURES

Sister Act 2: Back in the Habit
(1993)

TELEVISION

As the World Turns
(1991)

On the Web

Lauryn Hill has become a darling of the Internet with literally hundreds of websites chronicling her life and career. The following are some of the better websites serving Lauryn Hill.

Lauryn Hill—
This is the official website of Lauryn Hill's The Miseducation of Lauryn Hill. *It features audio clips, lyrics and an okay but overly fawning biography. Its strongest element is an up-to-date news section that gives the impression of literally being at Lauryn's back at all times.*

http://www.laurynhill.com

Beautiful Black Women Online: Lauryn Hill—
A solid photo gallery that showcases Lauryn Hill in all her natural beauty.

http://energy4life.com/BlackWomen/LAURYN
HILL/index.htm

E! Online Music Review: *The Miseducation of Lauryn Hill*—

For a quick introduction to the album, this site offers a review and selected audio clips from the disc.

http://www.eonline.com/Reviews/Music/Leaves/
0,6,921,00.html

Imusic: Lauryn Hill—

A quick and concise biography.

http://www.imusic.com/showcase/urban/lauryn
hill.html

Lauryn Hill—

A thoughtful essay discussing her music and career.

http://www3.sympatico.ca/mr.exe/Lauryn.html

Lauryn Hill—

A series of photos of Lauryn and the lyrics to the songs of The Miseducation of Lauryn Hill *highlight this site.*

http://www.angelfire.com/ak//Psyca/Lauryn
Hill.html

Music Boulevard—

A collection of features and reviews that will get you up to speed on Lauryn Hill and the success of Miseducation.

http://www.musicblvd.com

NJO: Spotlight on Lauryn Hill—

An entertaining mixture of news items, sound clips and a forum chat line.

http://www.nj.com/spotlight/hill

Sonic Net Music News—

Easily one of the best of the bunch, this site contains a biography, photos, up-to-the-minute news, a discography, audio clips and concert and album reviews.

http://www.sonicnet.com

The Fugees Website—

A fun, multimedia look at the Fugees's universe.

http://www.music.sony.com
http://www.fugees.net/fugeesindex.html

The Unofficial Fugees Page—

Pictures, audio clips and video clips make this site a must-see.

http://user.aol.com/Snicka/store.htm

The Nick's Page—
A good collection of audio clips and pictures.
http://www.geocities.com/Hollywood/Lot/1861/